FEARFUL
PLEASURE

Also by P. A. Chawla

The Slow Disappearing

Mumbai Mornings

The Shenanigans of Time

FEARFUL
PLEASURE

P. A. CHAWLA

Pen-N-Mouse

For information contact: info.pennmouse@gmail.com

First North American Edition: May 2024
Not for sale in the Indian continent.
Cover artwork created by Petals Publishers
Printed on acid-free paper.

Library of Congress Control Number: **2024909347**

ISBN: **978-0-9888221-6-0**

For D

Bye bye love

Bye-bye happiness

Hello loneliness

I think I'm gonna cry

Bye-bye love

Bye-bye sweet caress

Hello emptiness

I feel like I could die

...

Lyrics by The Everly Brothers

Foreword

I have not met Ms Chawla personally. Yet, I feel as if I know her intimately through this book. The push and tug of her characters, her meandering but strategically driven plot lines, her capacity to tackle with the clear eye of a seer, and no embarrassment whatsoever, the subjects that either interest her or affect her most deeply say a lot about the person behind the book.

One thing I have understood about Poonam is that for her, as a writer, no subject is off-limits – adultery, incest, promiscuity, ambition, love, honour, humour, loyalty, or any other subject. She is sorted inside out as a writer. When asked, she says every human being is capable of goodness and evil in equal measure. She is an excavator of emotions. Well, talking about this particular book, I think - the author behind "Fearful Pleasure" plays the role of the good, the bad, and the ugly with equal conviction. It is frightening how easily she slips into each personality. One might say, she is a little schizophrenic.

How would I describe Fearful Pleasure? Is it an elegy? I am not sure. A confession? Again not sure! But surely, an arrow of pain piercing through the predatory, persecutory, power-driven nature of man, to come out trembling on the other side. Or maybe all of the above.

And yet I read the whole book easily in one sitting.

Ms Chawla does not discuss race or class or the socio-political climate of the time. But that is not to say she lacks an understanding of class differences, the patriarchal structure, or cultural norms. They form the patina of this fearfully pleasurable tale.

In short, this is a book about a girl who comes from a broken home and seeks refuge and repair in marriage. Of course, there are no easy fixes. But despite the importance of this subject matter, this is not just a book about teenage depression and suicide. It is about survivor guilt and adolescent crises. It's about predators who walk free, about marriages that last a lifetime, and men who crush you under their weight. And finally, a way out of the tunnel.

The secondary characters are well-rounded and hilarious. You can tell Poonam was born and raised in India although she now resides in the USA. Her knowledge of the sexual shenanigans of maids and watchmen, the superstitions that plague the working classes, and the insecurities of housewives are all captured with humour, sympathy, and yes, even love. This book is a resounding yes.

Vinit K. Bansal
Author and Editor

New York

There were a great many things he did not
know about his lover.

One

It has to be a beautiful day. Sami Solanki thought idly, even though the warmth of the sun offers no solace to a body on its descent into the earth, the vagaries of weather, like the vagaries of men finally beyond its concern.

How strange, she mused, that she could see herself lowered into a casket, her face, the colour of corn husk, her body stiff as wood, and not laid to rest on the funeral pyre according to Hindu custom.

Yes. Definitely, a bright, sunshiny day, she brushed her hands with the resolve of one moving on to other matters and smiled up at the heavens, certain she saw an agreement in the gently bobbing clouds. Then she watered her hydrangeas, watched them sway, drunk on celebratory light.

She felt for them, you see – for Martin, for the neighbours in Westchester County, clambering fuzzily out of bed, asking each other *where exactly is the funeral, honey?* For her colleagues in black armbands hastening out of meetings, anxious to beat traffic on their way to the services.

Sami's eyes welled up. To have blue skies meet and greet the solemn party hovering respectfully over her - the woman with the sad, tumultuous eyes – what more can a body want?

At the funeral services, she can see them now, men and women, sighing inwardly, adjusting their bodies so that they are comfortable, hands folded on their laps, until someone, perhaps Martin, attempts the perfect eulogy.

Sami has heard a few eulogies in her time and admired the mourners who stood before the grieving family, and struggling through the fog of loss, raised their voices in song, or borrowed from the immortal words of Milton, Gray, or Tennyson, to soften the blow of death.

In death, if not in life, it should be mandatory to receive at least one speech that proffers more than a polite handshake or passing approval. A pitch-perfect speech that begins with trembling lip, gains momentum with praise, soars with philosophical sentiment, and winds down with ragged breath, the last words, like the rhythm of rain, lingering dewily, making the very air glisten.

Is there an App for eulogies? Sami wondered briefly before she did a Google search on her cell phone. Of course. No surprise there.

So, having picked a day awash in light and laden with hope, it made sense to also arrange in advance, for a perfect brunch of buttered biscuits, powdered doughnuts, and croissants with chocolate cream for the wake. And plenty of cold chicken sandwiches and potato salad. Whoever created potato salad with bacon bits, almost certainly had a wake in mind, Sami thought. They were so hearty, so right – sustaining and not overly festive with confetti-like bits of bacon.

And after they were done celebrating her life, the bereaved could wrap an extra sandwich in a dinner napkin, or pile some leftover salad in a baggie, wipe the powdered sugar off their lips and perhaps take off for a spontaneous drive to the nearest beach to watch a frenzied game of volleyball and get the taste of death out of their mouths.

But why on this the happiest day of her life was she dwelling on death? Sami had a face to prepare, a wedding dress to slip into. A union to legalize. No band. No *baaja*. No *baraat*. The Botox injected three weeks ago to ease the pain in her leg, was working.

She would don her dress and stand tall and proud next to the blushing Martin. Sami tasted his name in her mouth. Warm. And sweet as honey.

You owe me five farthings, say the bells of St. Martin's, she caught herself humming.

After the wedding, they would set off for brunch in Martin's car. His mother, his sister, and his son Patrick, age seven.

A bunch of Martin's friends would meet them at McLoone's, a restaurant, she privately thought, with a very unoriginal menu. Martin had chosen the place for the view. And because he liked their crumb cake. Two women she knew from work might show up and of course her hundred-year-old friend, and his caretaker.

Surely you know more people, Sami? You've been here for six years! Martin had asked, perplexed.

"No," she'd said, "I don't know anyone." Outside the sun smiled like a used car salesman. Too much. Too long.

Together, you will be singularly happy, it said, shining directly into her eyes. Yes. Until we separately die. Sami thought. There was a knock on the door.

Lynn knocked once. Then again, after a discreet pause. It was Sami's day. She must be nervous. Of course, she must be. Lynn was too, although she was not sure why. Maybe she should have asked Emily to drive down with her, she sighed. But Martin specifically asked that she go alone, without his sister.

"Be a mom to her today, Mother, could you? She has no family here," he'd reminded her.

The first time he brought her home, Lynn was both pleased and relieved. Pleased because he hadn't given up on women, or taken to lurching home at odd hours, traces of vomit in his hair – Lynn believed that no grown man could handle divorce like an adult – and relieved that Sami was clearly not his type. Lynn wanted Martin to be happy. Naturally. He was her first-born. Everything, everyone else came second.

But she also believed in timing, moderation, and a feeling of rightness that came partly from the gut and partly from simply having lived longer. And she was afraid it was not yet the right time. The air was still rife with tension in Martin's home. And Patrick, his poor boy, thrashed about in his sheets, not asking for Barbara, his mama, not ever asking for anything but winding up in her bedroom, night after night, standing at the foot of her empty bed until he fell asleep on the carpet, curled into a ball, the ends of the coverlet caught in his mouth.

No. Patrick needed a kindred spirit. If not his mama, then someone who would stroke away his fears, warm him like a stuffed animal, tug at his ears to make him smile. This girl, Sami, was too solemn. No sense of humour was Lynn's first thought. Also, she was a brunette! Her son liked redheads. His ex-wife was a redhead. Martin called her Ginger. Or Carotene. And for a while, it was Chilli or Chilli-pepper. She had an infectious laugh and laughed often at his jokes. Sami, Lynn suspected, was not generous with her laughter.

Sami answered the door at last. Lynn took in her flushed face, the intricately embroidered white on white lace dress, with the deceptively prim high neck and full sleeves, so form-fitting, on anyone else it might look inappropriate. On Sami, it looked both sensuous and understated, youthful and elegant. Probably, the effect she had in mind.

"Very fetching," Lynn said. "My dear," she added.

"Not too tight?" Sami asked softly.

"You can afford to, with your body," Lynn said graciously. Sami rewarded her new mom with a smile.

As they walked down the driveway, Sami held Lynn's elbow gently. It was not clear who it was that needed support. Lynn remembered with a twinge of guilt, that she hadn't given the little speech she'd prepared, a sort of welcome to the family, you are my daughter now, etcetera. But in her defence, Sami hadn't asked her in, and a speech is not the sort of thing you bring to the front stoop like a casserole, after all, she argued. It requires a setting. In any event, the girl looked so distracted, her eyes flitting about like someone who's been shaken out of a dream, it was better, thought Lynn, to take it slow. Get this part done. She had the rest of their lives, or at least until brunch, for a speech.

I love you, Martin. Was the extent of her speech.

They had driven straight to her apartment after a long day at work and made love. Afterwards, she was ravenous. They found a deli in Brooklyn, and ordered tuna on rye which they tore open and ate on the street, under a traffic light, using their napkins for plates.

She wiped some mayo off his chin and said, "I love you, Martin." Just like that. Then she went back to eating her sandwich.

There were many things Martin did not know about his lover. Like, what set off her limp. One moment she was walking like a gazelle, swift and proud, then, something she saw on the news, or on a billboard, or heard in passing, left her visibly distraught and limping.

Then, there was music, the tonality of certain pieces that triggered an inordinately emotional response. And the paisley shawl protected with cellophane that never left her travel case. Martin knew it must hold some special meaning for her. Not religious significance, he didn't think, like a hijab, or a prayer shawl, but perhaps a memory she could not forego. Was it a gift? If so, why was Sami not in touch with the gift giver? Her cell phone was always silent, her Netflix account had no added member, and her calendar was bereft of contacts. He knew this because they shared calendars.

Under the veneer of that familiar body, a body he had worshipped a thousand times, was a Sami he had not yet met. Martin wanted to unveil the real Sami, decode her like a work of art, cross the distance to her most intimate space, and fit within.

For now, he would settle for, "I love you, Martin." For her breathtaking sincerity.

Ah! Here she was, now! Tumtum ta tum. Tumtum ta tum.

When Grandma's car drove up and she gave them a big wave, his dad started singing, tumtum ta tum like they were real words he could dance to. Patrick liked his dad when he was like this. All happy and goofy. Then the car stopped, and Grandma was not the only one in there. She was there too - Sami. And the tumtum ta tum did not sound fun, it sounded silly. Like his Dad was putting on an act, playing the clown for her, or for Patrick, the way he used to when his mama first left because she needed time to think, she said and did not come back for a very, very long time, from her holiday.

Patrick thought Sami was real pretty. Then he felt bad like he was not supposed to think there was anyone as pretty as his mama. Mama had a big laugh and hair that sparkled in the light. She looked like one of those princesses in Grimm's Fairy Tales, that Grandma read to him when he was little - but not as girly. His mama always wore pantsuits. Sami's hair was dark, like an ever-growing night. Sami was very girly. She was kind and liked giving him presents. She was not so good at wrapping and pointed sadly at the way the paper stuck out at the edges. Patrick did not think it mattered. About the paper. Aunt Emily said Sami was trying to buy his love. He had no idea what that meant.

Tumtum ta tum! Here comes the bride! Dad dropped his hand

and rushed forward to take both of Sami's hands and swung them up and down and side to side like a real weirdo. She was smiling up at him like those women on TV when they see their war husbands at the airport. The ones that made Grandma cry.

Dad put one arm around Grandma and one around Sami. They looked like a family. Patrick wanted to get within their circle but not if they didn't want him to. He wiped his hand on his new pants. Then he counted on his fingers the number of weeks before he could be with his mama.

Two

He needs his mama, was Sami's immediate thought, when she saw Martin's son biting his lips, dressed in his Sunday best, the white shirt already coming untucked, his hair begging for a pat-down. Lynn found them a convenient parking spot and Martin dropped his son's hand to hasten toward Sami creating an empty space that made the boy look even younger, more vulnerable.

And so, despite his jocular tumtum ta tum and the cute little jig he did as he held out his hands, Sami's eyes still rested on the little boy whose mouth worked for composure.

"Hey, you don't look happy to see me," Martin half-joked.

She pulled herself together then, and held his hand with her own, letting Mama Lynn explain, "She's nervous Martin, it's a big day!" Then Martin put one arm around his mother and the other around Sami and they huddled together like a bunch of jocks before a big game, until Sami snuck her head over Martin's shoulder and beckoned Patrick, with a smile. Blinking rapidly, he took two uncertain steps, then walked them back, frozen. Sami, all too familiar with the tugs and tussles of the heart, let him be.

Emily, Martin's sister provided a little pageantry arriving in a smoking red dress, a tired bunch of flowers held together with twine in her hands and a slightly askew tiara on her copper-coloured head and Patrick innocently asked, "Are you getting married too, Aunt Emily?"

Then it was time for the ceremony. They kept their vows brief.

Sami said, "Martin, when I first met you, my hand recognized your hand, my heart remembered your heart and I knew why it was that I have always felt alone, and, need never feel that way again. With you in my world, I make sense."

And Martin said, "The day you smiled at me, Sami – Samar, I thought, just look at that smile! Please, God, let her choose me so that I may spend the rest of my days warmed by her smile."

Sami was glad he remembered to say her full name – Samar. And even as they looked deep into each other's eyes, she was skimming through the pages to arrive at the end of the story, where her character is being lowered into the earth and she was thinking: Yes. Let it be a beautiful day. When I die. A day like today. With plenty of sunshine. And no fuss.

At brunch, Sami glanced around the room, relieved to play a silent role, and only for a second did her heart stop. Was that...? No. It was no one.

The family Sami sought in every dark head and every pair of brown eyes was ignoring her, halfway across the world. For them, she was a spot on the map and aroused no curiosity. The most significant moments of her life were minor quakes, logged dutifully, unlikely to disturb the tenor of their lives. Nothing to see here folks. Go back to your homes.

"Are you okay?" It was Emily.

"Yes. Thank you." Martin rubbed her shoulders, massaged, and kissed her neck. Everyone went awww.

"Hey, you two, get a room," someone suggested boozily

Finally, it is over.

Finally, it was over. His dad thanked him for being the ring bearer. "Great job, buddy!" He said like Patrick had made a touchdown or something. All he had to do was hand his father the ring to slip on her finger. He is such a nerd, Patrick thought.

Sami looked as if she was lost in space. Patrick wondered what she'd have done if he went, Earth to Sami! Earth to Sami! Grandma once said Sami did not have a sense of humour. His mama would have laughed for sure. She laughed at all his jokes. She told him he had all her good genes. Aunt Emily was single, dad said. He supposed that meant she had no boyfriend. Which probably meant he, Patrick was single too. And so was Mama. And so was Grandma. We are all single, Patrick thought. Which was fine by him. It was peaceful.

At brunch, there were speeches and lots of laughing, and someone sang a silly song. His sausage tasted like gum. The pancakes were good.

Grandma told him Sami would come home with dad later in the evening. "She will live with us," she explained.

Patrick said, "Naturally, Grandma." And Grandma smiled as if he'd made a joke. But his heart was heavy and fearful. As if someone was leaving forever. Even though that wasn't true. Quite the opposite in fact. His eyes flitted around the room looking for dad. Looking for something.

Three

The way her eyes flit around the room, any room. As if she can't wait for it to empty or wait for it to fill with other faces. But who are these people she is looking for? Lynn wonders, not for the first time. Sami did not seem to know anyone in this country, except Martin.

Mama Lynn, she calls her. Martin's father would never have agreed to Papa Bob or even Dad. He was a bit conservative. God rest his soul. He would have denounced the girl, based simply on her appearance, or worse, for being a recent immigrant. As if there was a set period of time before an immigrant became acceptable – as if their complexions changed over time, faded to a more palatable paleness. Secretly, Lynn was relieved her husband was not around to judge Martin on the choices he had made. His divorce; his new wife. And Sami, Lynn thought, has so much pride. She would neither forgive nor condone an insult.

The Snow Queen – that's what her daughter, Emily called her. But then, Emily was not exactly crazy about Barbara either – Martin's Ex. Lynn pointed that out to her daughter, but Emily shrugged her off with, "That's, just my point, you like everyone!"

Which was not true. And even if it were, would that be so bad?

Except for a few, brief moments at the front door, when she came for Patrick or returned him to her care, Lynn rarely saw Barbara anymore. Their relationship was naturally strained. But at least she was still "Lynn" to Barbara. Still existed as a name and person outside the exigencies of her family. For that, Lynn would always have a place in her heart for Patrick's mother.

It was in her first trimester, when, to her quiet chagrin, Bob began calling her Mama. "Lynn" was cast aside, never to resurface again.

For everyone else in the family, she was simply Mom or Grandma.

Patrick lost his grandpa when he was just three. Lynn missed her husband, of course, she did. His absence was everywhere. But lately, at odd moments during the day, a sense of yearning took hold of her. Not for Bob, not even for the life they had together, but a longing to re-experience some pure, unblemished thing, some magnificent time or place she had no memory of. But how was that possible?

Perhaps, she thought, she ought to get away while she still had this feeling before inertia, or her aching back, tethered her to the patio chair, and a vagabond sun vanished permanently behind the night sky.

All our stories are recorded in the night sky, his father once told him. All you must do is look up at the stars to retrieve them.

Or maybe it was something he might have said. Our recollections change with time, with the telling and retelling of the past. What Martin vividly, certainly, remembered was that his dad often stood in the backyard, long after dinner was done and the kitchen light turned off and gazed at the stars, an unlit cigarette hanging from his lips.

Bob was a plumber turned sanitation inspector and not given to poetry. But after flashing a light all day into the bowels of public schools and city housing, perhaps the studded sky afforded him some relief, a glimmer of magic at the end of a tedious day.

In every photograph he had ever seen of his parents, Martin told Sami, Mom was looking into the camera, but his dad was looking at his wife, his fingers grazing her locks. They spoke about it once, he and his sister, how rare it was that their dad could stay so steadily in love, for such a long period of time.

"I love your stories, Martin," Sami said, her head on his shoulder, a star shining in each kohl-rimmed eye.

"Your turn. Tell me something about your family. Your life in India?" He prodded. Martin felt her stiffen and unfold within his embrace.

"I need to get my shawl," she said quietly. He released her, while still looking into her eyes. Sami averting her head, hugging herself, walked swiftly toward the house, her limp re-appearing as surely as if someone had flicked a switch.

Martin stared after his wife, then turned his attention to the night sky, thoughtfully, wondering if he and Sami would hold on to each other for as long as Bob held on to their mother.

The way he held her, the way she felt when he gathered her in his arms, Sami wondered if that breathless feeling would disappear one day, go the way of dreams. She turned the closet light on and stood still for a moment. Slowly she exhaled. She stood on her toes to get to the box on the shelf, above the cramped row of dresses. She found it, right on top of the sweaters, laundered and neatly folded. Sami stroked the shawl, traced her fingers over the paisleys, held the fabric to her nose, and sniffed. The smell, indefinably Indian, was quite gone. She wrapped the shawl around her shoulders and stared at herself in the mirror. Am I really married? In the mirror, her eyes stared back, dark and afraid.

Married without a priest, without a havan, without the presence of a sacred fire. Where are the words of wisdom from the elders, the propitiations to the Almighty to keep you safe, healthy, fertile, and fruitful? Where is the send-off from Amma with sodden cheeks, and Babuji's tender blessings?

Married. Ha! And so, it raged, an internal dialogue that coloured her every blessed moment in monochromatic grey.

Soon Sami would go back out to look at the stars. Her husband might still want to know some interesting little tidbit about her past. If only, she sighed, the past could be swept off like debris with the rain, making the path seem more inviting, not quite so murky. If only they could build new memories, without disturbing the old.

Sami readjusted Amma's shawl and hugged it close. Here was Martin with stars in his eyes. Her heart leapt up. This might still work out.

Four

This might still work out, Lynn told herself.

Often, she sought comfort in her mother's last words – all endings are tragic, Lynn, she said, but then come beginnings. Don't grieve for too long.

Lynn forgave Barbara for destroying her son's happiness and encouraged Martin to do the same. She was not a bad woman, Patrick's mother, nor was she unloving. But it was as if there was only so much space in her travel bag and love for her child had to be compressed into a single packing cube so that she had enough room for all other essentials. No one thing was less important.

Barbara visited Patrick when the conditions were right, and the stars aligned. Sure, she could still charm the pants off him with her booming laugh and her goofy games. But then she left him staring after her, hope and fear tugging at his heart in equal measure.

He was seven now, still hopped from one foot to the other when he heard from his mother, but lately, Lynn noticed a little hesitation in his tread, making the walk to the front door seem longer. Lynn remembered how he once flew into his mother's arms, an irrepressible cyclone. And it broke her heart.

Oh well, Lynn sighed, Martin is married now, again, and Patrick does look happier. A hundred years from now, none of this will matter. At all.

Five

Sami knew she had to see the 100-year-old-man sooner rather than later. After all, time was not on his side. She bit back a smile, aware of the irony, and began to dress carefully, in the youthful colours he so enjoyed.

Once on the parkway, her mind drifted to the first time she met her centenarian friend. He was being rushed to emergency care, she remembered. There was a knock on her door, she'd hesitated to answer because she had been crying into her ramen bowl and didn't want anyone to know. But the knock was followed by two, short peremptory rings. Sami took one look at the harried woman, her clothes thrown on in obvious haste, her breath ragged, and asked, "Can I help?"

"That's why I'm here. Please come down with me. Emergency Services will be arriving any minute." Sami followed the no-nonsense woman who introduced herself as Mrs Mistry on the way to the lower floor and followed her into the apartment. Mrs Mistry had left the doors open with her doorstopper.

"This is Mr…"

"I was one hundred years old in June! Still going strong! You, see?!" A toothless person, apparently prone to speaking in exclamation points, grinned up weakly at her.

"Calm down and use your oxygen mask. If nothing else, it is

your lack of reverence for the thirteen other punctuation marks that will drive me to the asylum. Now, let me dress you, Old Man," Mrs Mistry said spiritedly, then turned to Sami, without pausing for breath,

"Will you watch him, while I get his documents and overnight case ready?" And, disappeared into the recesses of the house. Sami did not get his name – Mrs Mistry, with the ease and familiarity of a long-term companion, addressed him only as Old Man and never got around to introducing them.

When he returned from the hospital, excited he was still alive, punching the air with childlike joy, Sami decided to befriend the gnome of a man and in the months that followed, began to cherish his company.

Sami realized with alarm she had arrived, with absolutely no memory of having exited the parkway or of taking the jug handle to get to the old man's apartment complex.

She picked up the flowers she'd bought for Mrs Mistry, and the Burberry cologne he loved and walked the two floors up to his apartment. "Here she is!" The door opened before she had time to knock.

"Hi there, Mrs Mistry..."

"Where is your *sindhoor*?" The gnome shouted from his rocker.

She leaned down to give him a hug, trying not to look as if she had been punched in the stomach.

"His name is Martin. He's white. They don't believe in *sindhoor* and stuff," she said quietly.

"Then I don't believe you are married." The 100-year-old-man said querulously.

"Don't be rude, Old Man! Do you want to lose the only guest we ever have?" Mrs Mistry buried her nose in her flowers and smiled her thanks.

19

"I'm sorry we couldn't come – the Old Man was in ER again."

"I don't want to talk about it!!" The gnome shouted.

"I will wear the *sindhoor* from now on," Sami said, patting his shoulders. The 100-year-old-man smiled his toothless approval.

Upon her return, she was tired and restless. Martin, sensing her shift and turn in bed, held her close. Then she was wide awake, waiting for dawn, thinking about the 100-year-old-man and her promise that she would apply tradition, in the form of a red powder, in the centre parting of her hair.

Propping up on one elbow, she watched her husband sleep, the soft hair on his chest curled and damp with their exertions. She counted with wonder, the number of days she was married. Once upon a time, she had lain on another man's bed. She could map out the route she took from her bed to his. Sami shuddered involuntarily.

Still, here she was.

How strange that she had to travel over land and sea, to find a corner to sweep, to adorn with habit, and call it home. "Hey! I love you," she breathed into her husband's ear.

"Hey!" Martin whispered; his voice still heavy with sleep. Sami stepped out of the labyrinths of the past, with a soft smile and pretend yawn.

"Go back to dreamland, it's Sunday," she said, walking her fingers down his chest.

He raised his hand, touched her face, lightly. She closed her hand upon his, unwilling to let it slide to her breast and draw her closer.

She needed to empty her head first.

Soon he fell asleep again, little puffs of air escaping through flared nostrils. They now lay side by side, her hands crossed in front of her, eyes on the ceiling, as if positioned for an open casket funeral.

Sami stared up at the ceiling and wondered whether Amma too, in her solitary bed, stared up at the ceiling fan whirring above her head. What did she think? Did she imagine her daughter in a foreign land, sipping coffee, adjusting her scarf, looking on both sides before she crossed the street … and send out a loving prayer to Narayana, the god of second chances?

Does my absence sit like an unlit stove in the centre of your heart, Amma?

And whether Babuji, driving around the city he loved, saw his little girl's shape in the columns of smoke rising out of the chimneys of tall buildings.

Does the house feel silent without your daughter, Babuji? Deafened, like ears after a bomb blast?

And Atal, her little brother, her Cheetah, did he move on to happier pastimes – video games, cricket, surreptitious texting with the girl next door? Or did his bike, on its own accord, steer him in the direction opposite the cricket grounds, to the neo-colonial library, where he roamed the halls looking for his sister in the dog-eared books she voraciously consumed – Little Women and Catcher in the Rye and The Old Man and the Sea?

Cheetah, do you miss our games as well? And if you do, why then, is my phone still silent?

Stop it. Just stop it. Sami scolded herself. Once again, she turned to face her husband.

"Hello." He smiled.

"Tell me." She whispered.

"Tell you what?"

"Tell me, I am yours."

"I'm yours," he smiled and pulled her close. Martin couldn't get enough of this honeymoon haze.

Six

They did not go away for the obligatory honeymoon. Sami didn't think it was necessary. And she was right. They had silk sheets. A king-size bed. Ice cream and kebabs in the refrigerator. Patrick was with his mama for the weekend. The day unspooled before them, rife with possibilities.

Lazy days. Lustful nights. He sang making her grin and blush.

"There is one thing I'd like us to do this weekend ..."

"Pray tell," he said, grabbing her foot.

"No... no... idiot, that's not what I meant."

"Are you sure? Not even ..." his hand moved up her leg.

She was in the shower when he went down to get breakfast started.

Sami tugged at the floral chiffon so that it fell precisely two inches below her ankles, just skimming her heels. She turned this way and that. The inner skirt, or petticoat as they called it in India, seemed to have a mind of its own, edging out, ruining the effect. Sami lengthened her saree another half inch, smoothed it in place, and was satisfied at last.

Martin, his mouth full of peanut butter and orange jelly, rose, almost knocking down his chair.

"What are you doing? Don't get up," she scolded. He pulled out a chair, and waited for her to sit.

"I was just... You look like a princess, a queen."

"Hardly, it's an old saree, older than I am," she muttered, clearly pleased.

"Do I need to change?" He looked down at his jeans, hastily clearing the crumbs off his jersey.

"No. You look good. Great. I have to do this, for someone we are meeting. I mean, I just met them last week, but we need to go together. As a couple. It's important. You don't mind, do you?"

"Of course not!" Martin could barely contain his excitement. Maybe she is not the lone survivor of a long-lost tribe, or an avatar descended from some Indian heaven, after all.

"I am not allowed Indian sweets. Too much sugar! Do you want to kill me?" The gnome shouted in greeting. Martin, taken aback, looked to his wife for a cue.

"They are not for you. They are for Mrs Mistry." Sami put the mithai boxes on the hutch and bent down to kiss a shiny spot on the hundred-year-old man's head.

"This is my husband, Martin." The gnome nodded and fixed her with a piercing look.

"You wore *sindhoor*! You are married! Good!" He exclaimed and gestured toward the frayed leather loveseat. "Sit. Sit."

Mrs Mistry was unexpectedly reticent. Almost nervous. She kept patting her hair in place.

Finally, she took Sami aside, to the kitchen. "What shall I serve? You know how we live. We never have guests," she said running a tongue over her upper lip.

"Really, Mrs Mistry, we are absolutely fine. Besides, it's only Martin. Here, let's make some tea. Shall we?" Sami put the kettle on.

Mrs Mistry disappeared into another room for a few minutes. When she returned, she looked shy.

She placed a red scarf with an exquisitely embroidered border, in Sami's hands, blushing prettily, "I wish I had something more modern to give you, but this is a piece out of my wedding saree. I hope you like it. The Parsee border, see?" She passed her fingers over the delicate embroidery.

Sami inordinately moved, examined the scarf, and wore it so that it covered her hair, leaving the ends free. Then with an arm around Mrs Mistry, she ordered, "Martin, a photograph please."

Unexpectedly, Mrs Mistry planted a kiss on her forehead.

"We will be leaving now."

"..."

Sami leaned closer. The gnome opened his eyes and much to her consternation, began weeping.

"Bulbul. Bulbul." He sobbed, soaking the front of his shirt.

"It's his granddaughter ... Bulbul. He's been missing her lately. Perhaps, he's reminded of her, seeing you in a saree?" Mrs Mistry explained.

"It's okay Old Man. It's okay."

"You are my granddaughter? Bulbul?" The hundred-year-old man stroked Sami's face anxiously.

"Yes. I am. And you are my Babuji." Sami wept.

At the door, she turned to Mrs Mistry and kissed both of her hands.

Mrs Mistry apologized, once again, for not attending their wedding brunch. "He was in the ER again. I really would have loved to come." She sounded momentarily resentful.

They nodded, understandingly.

On the drive home, Martin looked at his bride, wet-eyed and wistful.

What is her story? Martin wondered. What the heck is her story?

Mumbai

Pieces of her past

Seven

Babuji eyed the scum settled resolutely on the surface of his teacup, with palpable dislike. She's been heating and reheating the same damned tea, he muttered under his breath.

Next, he looked at his plate, with the remnants of his fried eggs and ghee-rich parathas still sitting on the side table, now providing a repast for some very malevolent houseflies.

"Radha. Radha!" He called, with incremental dismay. Babuji did not like raising his voice.

"*Jee, ayee!* Coming!" Babuji winced.

How often had he told his family and staff alike, to keep their voices down? This was his home, not a dog pound, he often said, raising one finger like the Judge that he was.

The maid, Radha, huffed in and stood biting her lower lip, awaiting instruction. Babuji looked pointedly at his plate, tilted his chin at the offending cup of tea.

"Shall I take them away?"

"If you would be so kind," he said between his teeth. "And please ask Madam to make a fresh cup of tea. With her own hands this time," he stressed.

If Radha was insulted, she certainly did not show it.

"Yes, Babuji."

Perhaps I should interview the staff myself before she inflicts such miseries upon me, he thought, particularly displeased with the intellectually challenged Radha. But he discarded the idea almost before it took shape. Babuji knew his wife well enough not to cross her territory.

With the room cleared to his satisfaction, he lovingly gathered his stack of papers including the Mumbai Times. Babuji loved Saturday mornings. It was the only day in the week he allowed himself to have breakfast apart from his family, sip innumerable cups of tea, and do his reading.

Only after he'd harrumphed over the newspaper headlines, perused the comic pages, and laughed heartily at the political cartoons did he brush away imaginary crumbs and place the newspaper on the side table with the air of a missionary introducing The Book of God to a recent convert.

His daughter Sami was usually the first to wander in, still rubbing the gound out of her eyes. She split the pages so that she kept the politics and Bollywood sections and passed on the sports and comic pages to her brother. Hours later, the newspaper, a little muddled and worse for wear, found refuge in his wife, Kamla's bedroom, where she timed herself for a six-minute read every afternoon when the heat made it impossible to do anything else. Kamla did not believe in allopathic medicine and usually looked askance at home remedies but when it came to the soporific properties of the news, she was a believer. And she was right.

Somewhere between a rambling preamble and the empty promises of a Party Leader's speech, her bifocals slipped off her nose, and just like clockwork, she was asleep.

Babuji rubbed his hands with anticipation eyeing the weekly mail tied loosely with a bit of twine. He opened, no, unwrapped each letter like a gift, gave his full attention to each missive, and having read it, immediately set to work, framing his response. Only after he had sealed and stamped his answering communication, did he move on to the next. And the next.

That Saturday, he recognized his sister's handwriting and saved her letter for last, as a special treat.

First, Babuji shut his study door, so that he may reflect upon his sister, that fierce ball of energy under whose shadow he shyly grew, a delicate sapling, fearful and thrilled. Holding his breath like a child, he slit open the envelope with a Papier-Mache letter opener. Tearing it would be a desecration.

He read her cryptic note. Then read it again.

An hour later, he went into the sitting room. His wife glanced up from her embroidery, took one look at his bloodless face, and rose, letting her work slip off her lap. Babuji hesitated. That should not be on the floor. Then flailing his arms as if overwrought, he left the room, with Kamla in tow.

Radha, the maid seemed overwrought. By now, it was fairly obvious that decision-making was not her forte. Surprisingly, Babuji had not yet relegated her from general maid to dishwashing duties. Or maybe, he was just biding his time. One never knew with the old man, thought Malik, the cook, nodding his head wisely, recalling incidents in time past that only he was privy to.

The maid stood in the hallway between the kitchen and the sitting room, scratching her nose. I have Horlicks to prepare, porridge to stir, spices to grind, she was thinking. But, she reasoned, surely Babuji's orders take precedence? So, she combed the house looking for Madam behind every door and when she found her at last, in the sitting room - instead of the bedroom closet, where she was usually seen fondling her jewellery, stroking her pashminas and generally behaving like the lady of the household - what puzzled Radha most, was the fact that Babuji too was there, standing over his wife.

Shall I still ask her for his fresh pot of tea, or has he already done so? Radha sighed miserably. She really did not enjoy getting into other people's heads. Perhaps this is why she was never considered for a management position.

It was a moot point, however, because, Radha, drawing up courage, had only just opened her mouth when Madam rose from the couch and followed Babuji back to his office, where they shut the double doors at once, leaving her gasping.

Radha placed her ears to the door. It was so quiet. I wonder what they are doing in there? Maybe the old man got restless and wants to fool around a little with his chubby wife? A giggle rose in Radha's throat as she imagined the old coot, coaxing his squiggly little member between his wife's jelly-like thighs and groaning as if he needed to take a piss, just before he came.

"Why are you standing there, giggling like a fool?" It was the cook, Malik. He lorded over the staff just because Babuji trusted him with the house keys when they went away on holiday.

Radha, the maid, shrugged and went about her business. But one aroused thought led to another and soon she was so hot, she had to hitch up her saree and skitter across the vegetable garden to the watchman's shanty. Finding him there, nursing a glass of tea, watching porn on his mobile phone, Radha, answered his smirk with a smirk of her own and proceeded to buzz around his nether regions for some delightful hanky-panky.

Kamla would not accept the fact that her brother-in-law was caught doing hanky-panky with his secretary. What was even more shocking to Babuji's missus of twenty-some years, was the idea, that his sister, Maya, did not believe in pleading with her husband, or reasoning, or perhaps even smashing some china. No, she simply walked out of her 2,500 square-foot home and into a hotel, dragging three suitcases and one nineteen-year-old daughter behind her. And here was Kamla arguing her case with Babuji, who was telling her, would you believe it, not asking for his wife's input, but telling her, in no uncertain terms, that things were about to change? That the spare room would no longer be spare and that his sister and niece were moving in!

Babuji, lips pressed in a thin line, waited for Kamla to stop ranting. His wife spoke almost exclusively in hyperbole. However, it was not her ability to remake the world into a stage at the drop of a hat that irked him, at that precise moment. It was the fact, that she was wasting time, instead of drawing up plans like any seasoned homemaker.

"My sister and niece are to live with us," he said finally when she paused for breath. "The decision is made. It is irreversible, incontrovertible, immutable."

At this, Kamla, generally a tractable woman, showed a side of her personality that shook him to the core.

"Ishhhh! How dare you use such big, fat words with me! Am I on the stand, do you think I did not understand your point, the first time!"

Caught in an avalanche of words, Babuji, who'd been married a long time became soft. Deferential. Guilt-ridden.

At last, Kamla succumbed.

Sami succumbed to the bribe and picked up her spoon with the air of a martyr. Of course, she still pretended to gag at the sight of the runny looking porridge, the apple cut up exactly the way she despised with the skin still on, and the toast with mango instead of strawberry jam, but the gagging was more for her little brother's amusement. Atal, imitating his sister's every move, followed suit.

Radha, the maid hadn't been working in Babuji's household too long, but she was the oldest of nine children and understood the way a kid's taste buds worked. Besides, she was not averse to gum and candy herself and once consented to having sex with a stranger based solely on the fact that he tempted her with a heavily sweetened betel leaf with a dab of pure tobacco, for her post-coital enjoyment.

This is why, seeing the pained look on Sami's face, she decided to ease her suffering somewhat, and whispered the magic words, "Eat this, there will be *chwingum* in your bag for later, Miss Sami."

Chewing Gum! What was she ten? Huffed Sami.

"If I was the teacher and you were in my cooking class, I'd fail you," Sami hissed.

"Me too," Atal agreed.

"Me three," Sami smiled.

"Me four," Atal giggled.

Radha continued to stand over their heads, her face now devoid of all expression except perhaps boredom. Her job was to watch and wait. The kids could not leave the table until breakfast was done. Every bite must be chewed and digested, Babuji always said, waving his finger in the vicinity of the digestive organs.

"Where's Amma?" Sami pouted when she was done eating. It felt weird leaving without Amma's hasty kiss and the usual caution – study well, stay out of the sun – before they took the bus.

"They are at it again," Radha whispered, huskily.

"I get it. You are trying to perfect your conspiratorial tone, for your acting audition," Sami responded with sarcasm. But it did worry her, this new compulsion on the part of her parents to go behind closed doors and discuss things at all hours of the day and well into the night. On the way to the school bus, Sami was still thinking about her parents' odd behaviour. It just did not add up!

Life in the Solanki household was a series of chores punctuated with carefully balanced cultural activities.

"Discipline was next to devoutness," Babuji said.

After a full day of loud-mouthed lawyers and foul-mouthed criminals, Babuji insisted on decorum. Domestic help must be soft-spoken, music must have rhythm, or it would be silenced, doors must be treated with respect – not slammed or pounded on as if there was a fire next door.

"Silence is golden," Babuji said. In keeping with the theme, even the décor was muted. White walls, plants stunted into submission, black and white portraits - occasionally in sepia, if he was feeling adventurous - curtains stiff as sentries shutting out the street.

"The background must stay in the background," Babuji said.

Sami saw the way Babuji winced when Amma rebelled against his instinct to dress her like a hospital wall. Instead, she made her appearance at formal affairs, like a terrarium of exotic, sherbety flowers balanced on high heels.

"Kamla." He would invariably mutter and click his tongue.

"Your taste is boring," she'd say.

"Boring is restful," Babuji would counter. "I recommend it highly, especially for Type A personalities, such as yourself."

"Ishhhh!"

So, it went on. Even their arguments were unchanging, predictable.

Suddenly, Sami stopped in her tracks. There had been one change in their unicolour lives, years ago, that was not snooze-worthy. Sami was nearly seven. Babuji was home earlier than usual which was, in itself, an unusual occurrence. But then there were sweets at the dinner table. Not *kheer* or *seviyan*, or any of those milky puddings, but actual candy - toffee and chocolate and all things yummy. Sami looked at her parents. Babuji was grinning. Grinning!

"Have some, Sami," he said.

Amma was looking coyly down at her plate. Sami took two and popped one in her mouth before he changed his mind.

"We have news for you Sami," he said. Six months later, they had Atal.

"Oh, my God!" She is pregnant, Sami covered her mouth with her hand. But of course, the news her parents shared with her on that same evening, had very little to do with cradles and lullabies.

Eight

Rock-a-bye baby on the tree top ... that was the first lullaby Sami sang to little Atal. Sami loved the baby the moment she saw him, swaddled in Amma's soft blue pashmina. Except for one pink ear, peeking out like a wingtip, his tiny body was completely hidden in the oversized shawl. Still, she decided, she loved him more than all her dolls, more than the blanky she dragged around the house ever since she mastered the art of walking - until it mysteriously disappeared at age six - more even than her best friend Amara and all her Lego sets, combined.

She was, in short, smitten.

Kamla, after a difficult delivery, still sore from a torn and bleeding perineum necessitating several stitches followed by haemorrhoids she was too embarrassed to mention to her obstetrician, allowed her daughter to visit her in her bedroom.

"You can play with your brother here if you like," she said, dejectedly.

Sami, surrounded by soft toys, was only too happy to soothe and sing to Atal for hours at a time, whilst her mother sought relief with sitz baths or lay on her back with a cushion under her tail bone.

Sami thought everything about Atal was fascinating. The way he sucked his toes, one by one, getting to know them all. The way he smelled, of talc and baby oil and breast milk. The way he moved his head, side to side like a bird until he singled her out from a sea of faces and pushed his arms up to be held. Atal, she would say, her heart full to bursting. Atal.

And Amma, despite her sleep-deprived eyes, would note the tender curve of her daughter's mouth and see the joyful wells in her eyes and catch her breath, and think, maybe she will be beautiful one day, the dark Amma, if she stays like this.

When he was eighteen months old and weaned off Amma's breast, Atal was given his very own room with a crib and a nanny.

One evening, Amma and Babuji left to attend a homeowners' association meeting, whatever that was. Amma wanted to stay back, but Babuji insisted it was time for her to go out and meet people again, she needed adult stimulation.

"If you finish your homework soon, you can look in on Atal, one last time before you go to bed," Amma said on her way out, smiling indulgently at Sami.

Sami was still working on her multiplication tables when she heard Atal cry. She listened for the nanny's sing-song voice and didn't hear any. Moments later, there was a fierce, urgent quality to the wailing that was impossible to ignore. Still, no responding noises from the nanny. Then, a few seconds reprieve, and another shriek, louder, heart-crushing. Atal!

For a few seconds, the sound of her feet thundering down the hallway helped stay the panic in her heart. The baby's room was partly open. He was, she saw, trying to clamber out of his crib. To Sami's horror, the moment he succeeded in hoisting himself up, grabbing the rails with his little hands, the nanny thwacked his knuckles with her fist making him shriek with pain. Poor Atal withdrew his hands, fell back in his crib. But then, reflexively, he tried again. And was thwacked again. Harder this time!

"STOP!" Sami lunged at the nanny with her entire body.

The woman, thicker than the eunuchs who came around for alms on the first of each year, barely moved a muscle. She smiled menacingly, then slammed her hand on Sami's chest and pushed her with such force, she fell flat on her back.

"Don't you even think of squealing on me, you little rodent, or I will stuff mirchi in his mouth the next time," she said, lifting her by the shoulder, her face so close, Sami could feel her stale breath on her skin.

"I won't tell. I promise." Sami gasped for air. She was shaking like a leaf.

"What are you doing here? Are you spying on me?"

"No. I just want to kiss him goodnight, before I go to bed," Sami sniffled.

The nanny strode out of the room with a warning glare.

The house was set back from the main road but the window above Atal's crib overlooked the driveway. Sami, now stunned into silence, oblivious of the pain in her chest, her shoulder, her head, waited by her brother's side, keeping her eyes peeled for Amma and Babuji. Her heart thudded in her ears. She reimagined the scene, this time with the nanny pushing fistfuls of hot chilli powder down Atal's throat, setting his tongue on fire, scorching his oesophagus, letting his precious body fold into a comma wracked with pain.

Her knees sagging beneath the weight of her fears, Sami heard herself whimper.

"Whatever is the matter, Sami?" Babuji held her up, alarmed. She hadn't seen them come in, after all.

"You left us. Alone! I hate you. I hate you both ... I hope you die!"

Sami's underpants were soaked. Her nose leaked. She no longer knew who or what she was raging against.

Babuji carried her in his arms biting and screaming. He thought it best to give her a sedative.

Just before dawn, Amma opened her eyes to a white-faced Sami, hovering by their bedside, shaking a fist.

"Either the nanny goes, or Atal and I go." Sami planted her hands on her waist. Any further discussion was pointless.

"Okay," Amma said.

"Okay," Babuji agreed.

On the following morning, however, the nanny was nowhere to be found. Perhaps it occurred to her that Sami was not as afraid of her as she might think, the way she lunged at her, like a she-cat, and despite her threat of causing bodily harm to the baby, might still complain. Besides, Babuji was a High Court judge and could probably throw her in jail without the slightest hesitation. In the end, she made her escape without worrying about her paycheck.

That evening Sami had her parents drag Atal's crib to her room.

"Sweet dreams, baby," she said, kissing each one of Atal's knuckles, now an angry shade of purple.

"We'll be fine now. Just the two of us. No one will hurt us here."

"**N**o one can hurt us here, I promise. And we will be moving in with your uncle, within a week. Do cheer up, Khushi, you are casting a pall on a perfectly pleasant day."

"Pleasant!" Khushi stared at her mother in disbelief.

"My father has committed fraud. *I will never be married.* He's run off with another woman. *I will never be married.* The police were at our doorstep. *I will never be married.* Pleasant, Mama!"

"All I mean is, it's not raining for a change and wasn't it a good idea to eat out on the terrace? And please, please, do not speak of your father and his transgressions, Khushi. Do you honestly think I need reminding?"

Despite all efforts to appear cool and collected, there was a crack in Maya's voice.

"I'm sorry. I just … I think I will go and lie down." But Khushi continued to sit, staring at her mother in her indecisive way. Guests at the boutique hotel, eavesdropping on the mother-daughter duo might reasonably conclude, that the daughter was incapable of making any decision, however small, without her mother's blessing. And they would be right.

On the face of it, Khushi had all the prerequisites for a sound partnership and, more importantly, for the somnolent life of luxury, she dreamed of - light skin, and not just light, but suffused with a roseate glow, as if just woken from a restful slumber with a lover's kiss; large grey eyes, so distinctive they immediately drew attention to her good, brahmin stock; a child's non-existent waist, and a simple, or shall we say a malleable mind.

The fact that Khushi had led a sheltered life and was barely past eighteen, also, had not escaped the attention of several aristocratic *ammas* shopping for a *bahu*. Already she had received a spate of proposals (some, directly from young men, champing at the bit, in the first flush of sexual excitement).

That is, of course, until her father did a runner with his secretary, who just happened to be another man's wife, and took with him, most of Maya's jewels and their combined savings.

Naturally, all marriage proposals were withdrawn, because no aristocratic family would shoulder a scandal unless it was sweetened with lots and lots of cash.

Who will marry me now? Became the doleful drumbeat driving out every other thought, making Khushi want to curl up with her face to the wall, her grey eyes greyer in the impending monsoon.

Maya nodded tiredly to her daughter, Leave, leave. For the life of her, she could not understand how any child of hers could be so ineffectual, so self-absorbed, so lacking in spirit.

She would have liked to lie down herself. Lie down and sleep eternally. Float in the cradle of Yama's arms where there was no past to regret about, no future to fight for. Where time had no meaning.

But she wouldn't give that cheating SOB the satisfaction of dying, she thought. That would be way too convenient. She had a divorce to file, damages to procure, blood to draw. None of which could happen, of course, until the absconding scumbag was dragged home by his balls.

Meanwhile, Maya believed, it was time to rewrite her story if she wanted a better life for herself and her daughter.

You are who you want the world to think you are, Maya recited to herself like a mantra.

"**O**m namah Shivaya. Om namah Shivaya. Om namah Shivaya."

The sweet, slow-cooked aroma of semolina roasted in ghee, pervaded Kamla's nostrils distracting her from her chanting. She tried one more time, then made the executive decision she had propitiated the gods enough for one day.

It was a big day. The Solankis were opening their arms and their home to Babuji's sister Maya and his niece, Khushi. But despite an almost visceral dislike for her sister-in-law, Kamla felt compelled to do her duty. Hence the prayers, the sweets, the fluffing of pillows, the turning down of beds in the guest rooms, the fresh soap and shampoo in the bathroom, and on and on. Naturally, everything fell on her arthritic shoulders. All her husband had to do, was keep a lookout for the cab and hold the door as they got out, with a clown smile on his eager face.

"Everything is ready, I hope you are satisfied," she said in a loaded voice, wiping her hands on her *pallu*, as she joined him.

Babuji nodded.

Kamla wanted more. A word, an acknowledgement. She rubbed her forehead with the back of her hand.

"The things I do for you... and to what purpose?" She left the sentence unfinished.

"You should do it because it must be done, Kamla," Babuji said. His sister, and her impending visit, propelled something roguish in him. Then he made it infinitely worse, by quoting from verse forty-seven, chapter two, of the Bhagawad Gita – You have a right to perform your prescribed duty, but you are not entitled to the fruits of action.

Kamla eyed him with hostility, swearing inwardly she would get back at him, the sneaky old manipulator! Under that absent expression, roamed a mind like a gold detector scouring valuable information from every hidden corner of the house – and of course, he knew, had held in his palm the information that it was verse 47 she was studying under the tutelage of her Guru – and flung it in her face when she least expected it.

"Ishhhh" was all she had to say to that. Babuji, in fact, the entire household was well acquainted with Kamla's deadly, nonverbal communications, comprising of huffs, whistles, spasms, and worst of them all, narrowed eyes.

This time, her Ishhhh trailed off into dead air, however, because a yellow cab rolled up to the carport just then and Babuji, quite forgetting his age and stature, ran down the stairs two at a time, to welcome his sister in a manner befitting a sister, rather than a permanent house guest with an inconsiderate amount of baggage.

Maya let out her breath, and helped herself out of the cab, smiling sweetly at her brother.

"Sri, how grey you look!" She said, passing a light finger on his temples. "Does that mean I've aged as well?"

"No. No." Babuji grinned sheepishly. He was uncomfortable with paying compliments, especially to the women in his family.

He turned to Khushi. "Come. Come out, Child."

Khushi sidled out of her seat and folded her hands with perfunctory respect. The watchman, astute enough to recognize a tip when he saw one, appeared magically and began offloading the cab, stealing glances at mother and daughter, assessing their affordability.

Maya did not see her sister-in-law at once, lost behind her brother's towering frame.

"Kamla," Babuji gestured, and his wife walked towards them, then stood stock still, almost in shock. Her sister-in-law, almost fifteen years her senior, looked half her age, she thought, despite her travel-weary appearance and ragged smile. Maya's saree blouse ended just below her breasts, revealing a pert little belly button. Her arms were muscular, her neck was long and bare, her hair was cut defiantly short, drawing attention to the solitaires in her ears. She wore no other jewellery. She is of a different world, Kamla thought, with a sinking heart. A world of gender equality and the spirited exchange of ideas. A world, I know little about. My husband's world.

"Welcome." Kamla managed, in a shaky voice.

Then Khushi stepped forward to greet her aunt and Kamla was struck dumb again. This girl. So prepossessing. Like a China doll. And so fair! Kamla glanced at her daughter and there too, she saw only inadequacies.

How common my Sami looks in the harsh light of the day.

Why can she not stay out of the sun? And must she always slouch?

Babuji bringing up the rear, glanced from his wife to his sister. He saw all of his wife's anxieties, her lack of self-esteem, her narrow, domestic upbringing coalesce into tiny beads of sweat dampening her upper lip.

I must be kinder to Kamla, he thought. My wife.

Khushi met Sami's eyes and smiled quietly. Sami nodded back. So, this is our new reality.

"And who is this?" Khushi bent down to tickle Atal, playfully.

Sami's hand flew to Atal's side, pulling him close. "He's mine," she said. "I mean... He is my brother, Atal."

Khushi withdrew her hands, wiped them delicately on her skirt.

Sami looked down at Atal. He was staring at his cousin, his mouth open, as if Snow White, The Mermaid, and The Princess Bride all rolled into one, had descended into his world like magic, an anime come true.

Still holding her brother's hand, Sami went to stand beside their mother. Together they watched a new era unfold.

Nine

And so, a new era begins, Maya thought, standing at the window, staring at the night sky, so vast without a moon.

She held an unlit cigarette between her fingers, not sure whether she ought to just go ahead and light it, it was her room after all, or at least it was the room allotted to her, or whether she needed her brother's permission.

I will ask Kamla, she decided, knowing instinctively, it was necessary to give the woman of the house the respect she was owed, especially since she was there for the long haul.

What if she can't handle it, seeing a woman with a cigarette? Maya sighed; bone tired. Kamla was a good woman, but she dwelled within these walls like a well-upholstered couch, and all she knew about other lives, not counting her clones in the neighbouring homes, was information garnered from the daytime soaps.

Of course, in the soaps, Kamla would play the righteous homemaker and she, Maya, flaunting her highlighted hair, parading her perky bosom, the happy home-breaker.

If only it was all so cut and dry, Maya thought, envisioning her husband, the rat, coupling with the Company dormouse, right this moment. Cursing audibly, she dropped the cigarette in her purse and stretched out on the large, comfortable bed.

This is a beautiful room, she looked appreciatively at the flowers blooming in the crystal vase, smelled the freshly starched sheets, and felt a pang of envy for the same Kamla she had derided just moments ago.

How nice it must be to live so purposefully devoted to one cause – the maintenance of home and hearth, the well-being of her family before all else. How uncomplicated and unconflicted her days, apportioned with self-appointed tasks – omelettes on Mondays, fast on Tuesdays, laundry on Wednesdays, picnics in the summer months, and sex on birthdays and anniversaries.

Kamla, Maya felt sure, had no quarrel with time or circumstance. She did not let the state of her body, with or without child, menstruating or menopausal, interfere with the demands of her family. Kamla did not clutter her mind with politics, lose her composure over poetry, discomfit herself with adulterous fantasies about younger or older men. Kamla probably 'ishhhh'd' in the face of such rubbish – what a wasteful expenditure of time and emotion! Maya could almost hear her say. Kamla had made her bed with her own pragmatic hands and was perfectly content to lie on it.

Khushi lay on her new bed, in her uncle's home, as content as one could be under the circumstances. At least, she was not being handled like a carry-on bag, dragged via public transport from hotel to hotel, trying to get as far away as possible from the sins of her father. And, she no longer had to share space with her mother.

Everybody has their own way of winding down before lights out.

Maya liked to read Elizabeth Barrett Browning's How do I love thee, then rail against her soon to be Ex – that lying, teaching, two-timing whoremonger – before she succumbed to sleep.

Babuji liked to make lists. The prosecutors he despised, the criminals he had sentenced going back fifteen years, the number of old, unopened, useless, items in the bathroom closet he would like to bin, and in what order, if his wife would only let him.

Kamla liked to have her legs massaged with scented oil, then roll over on her stomach for a back rub, before she slept. You can keep the rest of the scented oil, she would mutter to Radha, the maid after she was thoroughly moistened and relaxed.

Sami liked to imagine herself in 'smart' glasses. She saw herself as a teacher. Or a journalist, stationed in Libya, Morocco, or some exotic, dangerous sounding country. Smart glasses, it seemed to her, were almost a job requirement.

Atal imagined the joys of winning the lottery and what he would do with his money. M&M's milk chocolate candy usually topped the list.

Radha, the maid liked to rub herself with leftover scented oil she pocketed from Kamla's bedroom, then fuck the watchman, the last thing before going to bed. He made a great stand-in for her husband, on weekdays. On weekends, Radha went home to the village where she eked out an existence with the man she married. A man, who, to her everlasting regret, had only one testicle.

And Khushi, for lack of a husband, liked to pleasure herself. Naturally, she couldn't have her mother in her room to witness her nocturnal activity. The past few weeks, sharing the hotel suite had been particularly frustrating for Khushi, forcing her to take her naps earlier in the day, when Mama was out on the terrace, or in the lobby, flirting with hotel clerks. Keeping one ear on the door, you never knew with housekeeping, sunlight lasering through the blinds, it was all very rushed and guarded, and quite unlike the leisurely fantasies, she liked to play out under the cloak of darkness. But that was in the past. It's time to take control of my life, or at least, of my body, thought Khushi, and turned the light switch off in her very own bedroom with a decisive click.

"**I**'m going to turn the light off now, Atal, do you want to go to the toilet, one last time?" Sami clapped her book shut.

"Sami," asked Atal, "Isn't Khushi pretty?"

"Yes," said Sami, after a pause. "I guess she is."

Atal waited a couple of beats. "I think you are pretty too, Sami."

"Ha! I'm not fair though, am I?"

Atal looked her up and down. "No. I'm not fair though too, am I?"

Sami grinned. "You are my best baby."

Atal grinned. "You are my best baby."

"No. You."

"No. You."

Sami hadn't quite finished her homework essay as yet. She needed time to think. She set the alarm for 7 a.m. Perhaps if she rose early...

In school, Sister Doreen, quite forgetting she had done this exact exercise last term, said,

"All right. Let's use vocabulary words to describe MY FAMILY. Raise your hands, please."

"Dysfunctional," Maria said. Obviously, showing off.

They hadn't even learned the word yet.

"Nerve-wracking," Amara said.

"Fallible," Asma shrugged.

"Who isn't?" Sister Doreen smiled.

"Sami?"

"Yes, sister Doreen."

"Do you have a word to describe your family?"

"BO...RING," Sami had said, previously, throwing her head back and simulating a snore for the benefit of the entire ninth grade. And sister Doreen had tried to hide a smile.

Now, considering the events of the last couple of months, Sami changed her response,

"Complex?"

Sister Doreen looked at her searchingly,

"Indeed. Indeed, it is complex," she agreed and went on to explicate the pros and cons of the nuclear and joint family systems and the dynamics of inter-generational relationships. For once, Sami was intrigued.

'Family and what it means to you' became their homework assignment, due the following day.

Sami thought with residual sadness of her own family, now redefined as a joint or extended family with Auntie Maya and the lovely Khushi, in the mix.

A few weeks after they had settled in, Amma turned her focus on Sami, and in fact, became rather obsessive about dressing and grooming her daughter. At first, Sami paid no heed. She thought Amma was just being Amma and shrugged off her over-attentiveness.

Then she found the new bag of toiletries, placed prominently in her underwear drawer – a jar of Fair and Lovely cream, a pack of face bleach, a skin cleanser, and some astringent. Sami stared at the contents of the bag and swallowed the lump that rose in her throat. So, this was Amma's agenda. A magic potion that would make her daughter disappear and shazam return as a new, improved model – a Khushi.

Choking back tears, face flaming, she marched into the sitting room. Amma was working on a useless bit of embroidery.

"Fair and Lovely! You are hoping, what? That I will turn into Khushi?" Sami shouted, slamming the toiletries bag viciously on the centre table.

"What is the matter, don't you want to be pretty?" Amma asked with real surprise.

"Be pretty?" Sami was crying openly. "Am I ugly?"

"Sami?"

Sami jumped back, startled. She hadn't even seen Babuji in the room, hidden behind his newspaper.

"Babuji! Amma wants... Amma thinks..."

"I'm sure she means no harm, Dear," Babuji said, in his reasonable way.

"Don't speak on my behalf! Why would I want to mean her harm? Our daughter is dark-skinned – a blackie!" Amma raised a finger and pointed at Babuji as if pointing at a defective gene.

"I am just trying to help her." And failing. The disappointment was palpable.

"Well, at least, I'm not a fatty!" Sami's face contorted with rage.

Amma, blood drained from her face, chewed her lips, hands on her lap.

Babuji rose from the couch, held Sami's face with both hands, and asked, "Are you proud of yourself Sami?"

"That is your mother."

"And who am I?" Snot ran down Sami's face. "Who am I?"

Kamla lay buried under a blanket, in an attempt to muffle her sobs. If her own daughter thought so little of her, what must Maya think?

It never occurred to Kamla to examine the cruelties she flung at her daughter in moments of frustration. Nor did she stop to wonder why Maya seemed to pop into the equation so often, these days. Introspection was not Kamla's strong suit.

The sobs quieted down after a while, and she began feeling a little peckish. Of course, she could not go down to her kitchen, not after she had made a point of leaving her plate untouched, her hands in her lap, as the family ate guiltily, then left the table, first Sami, then Atal, thread behind her needle, and then Maya and Khushi, the two of them scuttling past Kamla as if she had an infection they might contract. Babuji had inched her plate coaxingly towards her, giving her no choice but to refuse.

Kamla tried to divert herself with some light TV viewing, but surely the universe was playing some sort of perverse game at her expense, because here was Master Chef Australia, cooking up a chocolate storm and there was Sanjeev Kapoor of *Khana Khazana* garnishing his *Rogan Josh* with a leaf or two of parsley, and the assiduousness of a Monet gilding his final lily.

Kamla turned off the TV, and decided she would go down to the kitchen, there was some leftover poha with her name on it and if anyone saw her, she would simply get a glass of water and bring it back upstairs. And tomorrow, she pressed her stomach with both hands sucking in her breath, tomorrow, her eyes filled again, she would start doing something about her weight.

Did Maya ever gain weight? How about when she was menopausal?

Kamla was still musing pensively when there was a knock at the door. It was Atal.

"Amma, I can't sleep."

"Where's your sister? Won't she tell you a story?"

"She says, not today."

Amma sighed.

"Okay. Get on the bed."

Atal, quite forgetting he was eight years and three months old, nestled in the curve of his mother's arm. The smell of talcum powder and Nivea pervaded his nostrils like a prelude to countless, gentle lullabies.

"Tell me, Amma." He said, eyes shining with anticipation, like Aladdin ready to take off on the wings of her sweet patois.

Kamla, putting aside her dire thoughts and hunger pangs, began her story with eyes half-shut:

'So, once there was a little boy, a grandmother, and a grandmother's helper. They lived together in a windblown house perched on wooden stilts and overlooking a carpet of green.'

"A boy, like me?"

'Yes. Like you. But, unlike you, the poor baccha was fragile – not very healthy. Every other day he got sick and had to stay home from school. The worried grandmother would sing to him until she had no breath left, and have her helper fetch him hot milk for his sore throat and cold compresses for his fevered body. Together the two old biddies nursed and soothed the little boy as best as they could. But just when they thought he was better, he got worse!'

"Where were his Amma and Babuji?"

'He didn't have any. One day they simply disappeared into the pages of a book and try as she would, the grandmother could not retrieve them.'

"Book? What sort of book?"

'A book called Kismet. And so, she looked after the boy all by herself.'

"She and the helper?"

"Yes. She and the helper. You are so smart to keep up with the story, Atal."

"What happened, next?"

'Well, one drizzly day in June, he was in bed, staring sadly at the tree outside his window, when he saw a brown sparrow dash across and plant itself on the tail end of a branch. How still it sat, the little bird, not heeding wind nor rain, like a bit of wood, upon the wood, eyes fixed into the distance! The boy called his grandmother and said: Look, the bird must be sick like me, or surely it would chirp or fly or at least look happier, don't you think?'

'Barely had the boy finished speaking, then the bird, as if hit by a bolt of lightning (even though there was no lightning) or by a heat stroke (even though it was a cool, rainy day) dove face down and fell to its death, right there on the asphalt.'

"OH NO!"

'Yes, that's exactly what the little boy in the story also said – Oh no! Then he turned to his grandmother and with eyes that looked emptier than the dead bird's, said: I think, one day, I will be struck down just like the little bird. And, with a sigh, he closed his eyes and went to sleep.'

'The grandmother wished him goodnight and went to bed. But I'm afraid, she got no rest – tossing and turning, and muttering 'there must be something I can do to give my grandson the strength to live. But what?' She had run out of medicine, and tears, and prayers. After many hours of worrying – she pulled at her scalp when she worried, and by dawn, her pillow was a net of hair – it occurred to her, there was one thing she had quite a bit of, and never put to use.'

"What, Amma?"

'Her imagination, of course! By the time the morning light danced on the lunette window of her bedroom, she had firmed up a plan. Impatiently, she rose the helper and told her what they had to do. When the boy woke up, he found his grandmother sitting by his pillow.'

'I spy with my little eye... something beginning with B, she said, smiling from ear to ear. It was a game her grandson had taught her, *and they both loved to play.'*

'The boy looked here, there, everywhere, then saw his grandmother shoot a furtive glance beyond the window.'

'A bird feeder! He exclaimed, joyfully. How did it get there?'

'It's a secret. Grandmother said.'

'And look, look how hungrily the birds feed out of it.'

'Oh! What a magnificent sight! He clapped his hands.'

'Eagerly, the boy watched the birds enjoy the sudden bounty and then fly off to spread the word. More of their feathered friends appeared, all day, every day, inserting their beaks in the miniature windows of the feeder. The boy was afraid the feeder might tilt and drop from the sheer weight of the birds, but it held steady. And when the birds flew off, it swayed ever so gently as if mesmerized by the song of the wind. This makes staying home almost bearable, grinned the boy, making his grandmother both laugh and cry. But Grandmother said: this here bird feeder is like an hourglass. I want you to know as long as it has food in there, you will remain alive and strong.'

'The boy's eyes widened. The birdfeeder was full to overflowing at the time. But would it stay full forever? Surely not. Perhaps because he was so full of joy or perhaps it was merely his good fortune, the boy felt infinitely better. He started going to school again and excelled at everything, from cricket to carpentry and even chemistry.'

"Cricket too?"

'Yes. Absolutely. And every morning and every night, he would gaze at the birdfeeder and note with relief that it was still full. Years passed. The boy became a man, strong, smart, and full of gratitude for the simple things.'

"Then?"

'Then one day ... his grandmother did not come to his room to draw the curtains and let him watch his beloved birds feed their bellies while

he got dressed.'

"What happened to her?"

'Old age happened... and death.'

" ....."

'The boy was saddened of course, but by now he was a man and knew, life must go on. So, the first thing he did, after he said his goodbyes was to summon the helper, who was much younger than Grandmother and still quite healthy. Haven't you forgotten something? He asked her, gently.'

'What would that be? She wondered.'

'The boy, (now a man) took her hand in his own and went down to the yard. There, a few yards from the tree sat two bushes so close together they could have been one. He parted the tangled web of scrub until he exposed the sack of hidden bird food. He dove his hands in and filled his pocket with the restorative seeds. Then he asked the helper to hold the ladder while he climbed close to the sturdy branch. With one hand he pulled the birdfeeder to his chest, and with the other, filled it with food.'

'When the bird feeder was filled to capacity, he clapped it shut. There. Only then did he look up at his grandmother smiling at him in the form of a cloud and said: See, Grandmother, I still live for you.'

"Amma," Atal asked, after a short, appreciative silence. "Did you tell stories to Sami as well, when she was little?"

"No. She... she didn't like my stories." Amma found herself struggling to explain. "Sami preferred conversation and ... not with me." But Atal had already drifted off to slumberland.

Kamla watching the sweet face of her only son, had an overwhelming desire to both cover him with kisses and perform a ritual to ward off the evil eye. Instead, she found herself distracted by the rumblings of her empty stomach. She merely sighed and rubbed her belly.

"I got you something... just a little snack." It was Babuji with a well-laden tray and his ridiculous bedside manner as if she was a patient.

Kamla did her best to look affronted, failed, then opened her mouth and allowed herself to be fed like a child.

When she was done eating, he quietly placed a page out of Sami's notebook in her hands and watched her face silently.

I wish I could disappear into thin air like a bird.

Kamla stared at each despairing word bleeding into the page, and closed her eyes, bereaved.

Ten

Maya spread a damp kerchief on her forehead and closed her eyes. She was listening to the sitar maestro Ravi Shankar. Babuji, or Sri to Maya, had assured her it was the panacea for her migraine. So far, it was not working.

Maya needed a job. Despite the high ceilings and sheer panels draped over the floor-to-ceiling windows, she felt caged in.

It's the suffocating routine, the inane chatter with her daughter, the having to worry about Kamla's feelings before she so much as poured herself a glass of wine, she thought, her blood pressure spiking. She wondered if she had made a huge mistake, agreeing to live under her brother's roof. We might be happier in a one-bedroom apartment in the centre of town. At least we'd be closer to civilization, Khushi and I, she thought, then grimaced.

She had no idea what made Khushi happy. The girl sailed through life like a paper boat, borne by the wind. Maya had enrolled her in the University, helped her with her course selection, even suggested extra-curricular activities - cooking instruction, music, art, Karate? Khushi had merely nodded in her lackadaisical way, "yeah, okay, whatever you think."

"There must be something you are passionate about? Hello, is there an echo in there?" She tapped her daughter's head, lightly. Khushi stared vacuously into the distance, twirling her hair around her fingers. The girl has no spirit, Maya thought aggrievedly. Sami

57

would probably tear my eyes out if I dared to provoke her. She remembered the unpleasantness of a few days ago, knew Kamla had said something to her daughter, something hurtful, and Sami had fought back, and never apologized.

Well, at least Khushi is attending classes now, Maya dipped her kerchief in the bowl of water at her bedside, squeezed the excess, and placed it back on her forehead. Her neck didn't feel as tight, and her migraine eased to a mere headache, about six on a scale of 1 to 10, and quite bearable, she decided.

Maybe, the club, she thought, quite out of the blue, or perhaps it was the bowl of water and the damp kerchief sticking to her skin, that brought to mind the posh swim and tennis club in the neighbourhood. Perhaps, if Sri finessed her a membership or a guest pass, she could get out there, relax by the poolside, even meet a few bigwigs, some evening?

Maya, with a degree in media communications from Columbia University and years of experience writing for tabloids, was certain she would be a good fit in the Television Industry. She was equally certain she would run into a celebrity or two by the club's prestigious poolside because isn't that what celebrities do best? Sit around a table, at a slight distance from the diving board so as not to get sprayed, and buy large drinks for pretty little ladies in their itsy-bitsy bikinis?

All she needed was a chance to drink with a bibulous celebrity (or two), thought Maya, after that, insinuating herself in their business would be easy as pie.

Yes, she thought, almost dizzy with relief, her headache now subsided to a two on the scale. Yes. Now I'm getting somewhere.

———⟡———

"Going somewhere?" Asked Kamla, sweetly. "I'm only asking so that I can instruct the cook..."

· "To the club, of course, Kamla, it is Friday," Babuji reminded her.

"Yes. I meant, Maya. Is she going to the club with you, then?"

"As a matter of fact, I am," Maya said. "Sri has invited me to join him, so I can get out of your hair," Maya smiled, the soul of good humour.

Kamla opened her mouth but could find no words. "Foof!" She expelled like an engine, falling back on the symphony of onomatopoeia. Babuji smiled into his sleeve and Maya merely smoothed imaginary fluff off her jacket as she stepped into the car. And they were off.

Kamla, in spite of herself, was pleased. Ah! To have the house to oneself. She cosied up on the couch, picked up her embroidery, and shut the door adjoining the kitchen. Then she turned her favourite soap on, adjusting the volume higher than Babuji would have liked.

But Kamla couldn't focus on the drama unfolding on the set.

What will she do amongst all those card-playing men? Babuji had never encouraged Kamla to join him at the club. Yet here he was, trying not to show his delight, chaperoning his sister.

Now, Kamla was chagrined.

But that was not the only reason she couldn't focus on her soap opera. Babuji may be the one with the eyes of an eagle, but Kamla too noticed things around the house. And lately, she noticed that Sami seemed particularly taken by Maya. Her cousin, the immensely attractive Khushi was, according to Kamla, far more qualified than her mother when it came to feminine graces, but, of course, Sami, probably to spite her mother, ignored Khushi and preferred to be mentored by the aloof Maya with her ridiculous bobbed hair and mannish pantsuits.

And now, Kamla was frankly upset. She was losing control over her family. It appeared, that neither her husband nor her children needed her anymore - because of course, if Sami would rather spend time with Maya, then so would her puppy, Atal, and she wondered whether she ought to do something about it or stay the course. In the end, she decided to stay the course. Instinctively she knew, there was a sense of comfort in coming home to familiar foods, common sense behaviours, unwavering positions.

Let them roam with Maya and get exposed to her highfalutin ideas, for now. In the end, they will come running back for my kitchen wisdom, she told herself, with righteous pride.

Besides, it's so hard to make changes at this age.

Kamla sighed with exhaustion. Managing her shifting moods was becoming a full-time job. Perhaps I will feel better after a snack, she thought, and pushing her orthopaedic socks up to her faulty knees, walked to the kitchen for a sizzling plate of onion fritters. Following on her heels was Radha, the maid, gingerly holding a cup of tea, doing her best not to let it spill onto the saucer.

Kamla set her plate down. Radha, the maid set the tea down next to it. Only then did they notice Khushi, standing by the window, unconsciously tugging at the tasselled ends of the curtain and looking especially lovely with that expression of melancholy she had perfected.

"Would you like to join me, Khushi? Some fritters?" Kamla drew her eyes to the plate.

"Okay." Khushi sat down, pricked a single fritter with a fork, and chewed appreciatively. Kamla stared at Radha, the maid until understanding dawned.

"I will get another plate," Radha said, and went back to the kitchen, sighing inwardly.

Kamla looked at Khushi.

A malicious thought crossed her mind.

If Maya was going to develop a relationship with her Sami,

perhaps she, Kamla, could get back at her and foster a relationship with Khushi?

"Uh, so, how are you?" Kamla tried. "Do you like it here?"

"It's a bit dull," Khushi said, still nibbling on her fritter, delicately.

"What would you be doing if you were in Kolkata?" Kamla asked, determined to be pleasant.

"Getting married," Khushi said, sullenly. Then she turned to Kamla with an expression so uncharacteristically animated, that Kamla was struck dumb.

"Do you know, Auntie, that I had three wedding proposals? I would've been married, living in a mansion somewhere, in Canada, Australia, but they all withdrew, when... after... you know."

Kamla tsk-tsked in sympathy.

"Yes. But you are so young. There's still time to think of marriage, isn't there?"

She certainly knew Sami's views on the subject. Her daughter's mind was affixed to education, then travelling to distant places, hiking, sightseeing, and living like the locals in places with exotic names like Phuket and Machu Picchu. "Marriage was just something other people did," she'd suggest, waving her hands as if pushing away her prospects, "People with little, or no imagination."

"Young?" Khushi was tugging the curtain, aggrieved.

"No. I'm beautiful right now. I know I am desirable. I see the way men ... people look at me."

The curtain dipped on one side.

Kamla looked as if she was about to collapse with shock – one did not, in her world, ever allude to men and their sickening desires!

"Auntie, can you not find me a man? So that I may be married?"

Khushi, red as a tomato, suddenly burst out.

Not yet in recovery mode, Kamla blinked and scrambled to get to the heart of the question.

Arrange a marriage. Is that what Khushi was driving at?

Kamla's eyes gleamed with sudden purpose. Here was someone, her gorgeous, grey-eyed niece, putting her future in Kamla's hands. And why not? Who else, but Kamla could pull it off? After all, it was her speciality – to act, get results without theorizing, and prevaricating, and weighing all options and assessing your strategies to death before you moved a single muscle!

All her insecurities poofed into thin air, and Kamla responded, almost giddy with delight,

"Yes, my dear. Why not? It will be my absolute pleasure."

The curtain fell.

No, not metaphorically. It took both Radha, the maid, and the watchman, to position it back on the window where Khushi was last seen, anxiously tugging.

Sami positioned herself by her bedroom window. She needed to keep an eye on Atal. There he was, doing his best with a cricket bat that reached his chin. Clean bowled! Someone yelled, as a wicket behind Atal, somersaulted to the ground.

"Idiot!" Shouted Austin, the team captain, then with obviously no spirit of sportsmanship whatsoever, threw his hands in the air and stomped off in the direction of his home. Soon the rest of the team dispersed, leaving poor Atal alone on the street, following them with his eyes.

Shit! Sami thought. Atal simply sat on the curb crying copiously into a white kerchief and of course, his sister would not have it. She ran down the stairs and immediately bumped into her mother, who almost fell backwards.

"Sami!" She clutched at her sleeve, trying to regain her balance.

"Amma! Baby's crying."

"What baby?"

"Atal, of course! Where are my slippers?"

"He's not a baby, Sami."

Sami stopped in her tracks. "Really Amma? We are splitting hairs, now?" She stuck her feet into her Keds, not bothering to tie her laces, and ran out.

"Hairs? What hairs?" Amma decided to ask Radha, the maid to give her an oil massage, it seemed her hair was splitting.

"Atal." Sami sat beside him right there on the curb.

"They left. They said I'm lousy. And a loser."

"And I say they are stupid. And not team players." Sami said forcefully.

But Atal would not be comforted.

"I'm no good at anything."

"Of course, you are."

"What, then?"

"Running. Each time I see you run, I think, Wow! He's like a cheetah. In fact, I'm not going to call you Atal anymore. I will call you Cheetah!"

"Really?" A smile hovered on Atal's lips.

"Truly."

"Truly?" Atal grinned, despite his glistening eyes.

"Really." Sami volleyed happily back.

Sami was on her way to her room, after settling Cheetah down with a tall glass of rose-flavoured iced milk.

"Sami!" It was Khushi. "Could you come here for a minute?"

Sami stepped into Khushi's room with more than a little curiosity. Her cousin had usually very little to say to her but to be fair, she didn't have much to say to anybody else, either.

"Yeah?"

"Do I look alright?" Colour rose on her neck.

She was wearing something shimmery in silver. It enhanced the grey in her eyes, remarkably.

"Stunning, as always. Why?"

"It's today. The big day."

"What big day?"

"Somebody's coming to see me, you see. Auntie Kamla arranged the whole thing ... and my mother helped, of course," she hastened to add, seeing Sami's hurt expression.

"Somebody?"

"A man. To propose marriage, didn't you know?" Khushi asked, amazed there was a world out there, chugging along, oblivious of this momentous event unfolding in her life.

"No, I didn't know. Yikes!"

"Aren't you going to stay and help your Amma with the preparations?"

"She doesn't need my help. Good luck!" Sami left the room abruptly before she said something decidedly unfunny about being put on the auction block, and sold to some Suit with multiple homes, including one across yonder hills.

Eleven

Sami was watching Notting Hill with her girlfriends.

The air conditioning at the Eros functioned sporadically, making her feel hot and cold in turn. Eyes on the screen, she reached for her bottle of chilled coke beading the floor of the cinema hall, at the same instant that Julia Roberts leaned forward to kiss Hugh Grant, in the fabled garden. A magical song stirred the verdure and wrapped itself around the lovers, and in Sami's heart rose an equal music.

Sami stepped out of the fug of the cinema hall and into the afternoon sun. Feeling a bit woozy, blaming it on the searing heat rather than the first stirrings of desire, she looked for an escape. A Cool Cab appeared at her feet, almost miraculously, and she dived into it, above her friends' protestations, (but you said you'd come with us to Café Coffee Day!) like one who has a secret she might spew without warning.

At home, there was the usual chaos before the entertainment hour. Amma was making scuff marks on the floor marching between the sitting room and kitchen, issuing orders to the staff; Radha the maid was running this way and that accomplishing absolutely nothing; and a houseboy was standing stock-still in the middle of the living room floor with a mop.

"Sami, there you are! Go check on your cousin. See if she is dressed."

"Why?"

Amma's eyes fairly bulged. "Go."

Sami knew very well why because Amma had circled the date twice with her red-tipped pen, that yet another highly eligible bachelor, along with parents, cousins and aunts was due to grace them with his presence, within the hour. She sighed at the monotony, the sheer ignominy of it – strangers drinking tea out of Amma's fine china, staring at Khushi as if she was the season's first mango, and proposing (fingers crossed) marriage if Ms Mango was found suitably lush, sweet and pliable.

Strangely, it was always Amma, not Khushi's mother (where was Maya, anyway?) who seemed more concerned about the outcome of these viewings.

Once the guests, after a last searching look at Khushi, said their goodbyes, Amma, like a diligent event planner, would critique her own work, what went right, what could have gone better. A marriage proposal, she firmly believed, had as much to do with a perfectly brewed cup of Darjeeling tea and the purity of the saffron in her puddings, as with the even white teeth and ivory skinned perfection of the bride-to-be. Perhaps there was something left to be desired in her brewing – although Maya would gladly have told her it was not the tea it was Khushi's absconding father and her SOB husband that was the problem. But so far, the mango, or rather Khushi, was found wanting.

Sami, still not quite herself after the momentous Hugh Grant Kiss, entered Khushi's room without knocking. Khushi was standing in front of the mirror, in a half-slip, but without a bra on. Her left hand cupped one breast. Suddenly, she put a thumb in her mouth and used it to wet her nipple, pinching and stroking it sensuously. Her face was flushed, her eyes half closed.

A wave of shock ran through Sami's body. "Uh," she said and backed out of the room. Thankfully, her cousin appeared not to have seen her.

Sami shut and locked the door to her room. She looked at her face in the mirror. Heat shot up her legs, spread dampness between her thighs. A cold film of sweat on the nape of her neck made her shiver.

Shaking off the images, Julia Roberts' lips on Hugh Grant, Khushi's thumb on her nipple ... she tore off her clothes and stood under the shower, not bothering to protect her hair. She was glad she'd locked the door. The last thing she wanted was Amma poking her head in, asking her why she was washing in the middle of the day.

Pressing a towel to her neck, and blotting and squeezing water out of her hair, she wondered, suddenly, what Amma would think of her pure-as-the-driven-snow niece if she knew how she spent her alone time. That would redress the balance, for sure, she smiled wryly to herself. Not that she planned to tell Amma of course, or to anyone else in the world, for that matter. Some things one kept to oneself.

Vaguely aware that something within her had changed forever, Sami, in an eyelet tunic and jeans, brushed her hair so that it fell in soft folds around her shoulders. Then she glanced in the mirror. Outwardly, at least, she looked exactly the same. As long as she kept a handle on the secret, suddenly fecund life in the folds of her brain, no one would be the wiser. Putting on an air of nonchalance, she ran down the stairs to help her mother feed the potted plants.

Fed on a steady diet of coffee grounds and flat soda, instead of water, every one of Kamla's plants bloomed in their earthen pots, exactly in the manner intended.

But as she stood snipping non-existent brown tips, two vertical lines marred the smooth perfection of Kamla's forehead. The Peace Lily, set on a polished, handcrafted high stool, its dark foliage spreading sedately above the living room sofa like an English butler, did its best to soften her mood. To no avail.

Where was Khushi? Kamla wanted her ready and seated casually on the couch with a magazine when guests arrived, so that she may project the image of a self-possessed, confident young person, ready to smile and entertain at the drop of a hat.

Lift your head up so, stand with the grace of a peacock about to display its feathers, then step forward and greet the guests ... Kamla wanted to tell her but did not. Khushi did not take well to instruction. Not that she was ever rude to anyone, and certainly never to Kamla, but she might simply shrug and nod her head in a non-committal way. Who knows, maybe this time, she might listen to me? After all, I'm only trying to improve her chances, Kamla sighed. She is soooo beautiful, but like all beautiful creatures, thinks she needs no improvement. I wish, she was more – she wasn't so – what was that word? Kamla sighed again, defeated.

"Amma... Why so lacklustre?" Sami broke into her thoughts.

That's it! Kamla thought. Trust her daughter to come up with the appropriate word, without even trying. Khushi had this look whenever people spoke of anything that did not pertain to her directly. She was just so uninteresting. So lacklustre! Kamla clamped a hand over her mouth as if she'd said the words out loud. Meanwhile, her daughter was still looking at her, askance.

"No. I'm fine. Do get dressed, Sami."

"I am dressed."

"So you are. So you are." Kamla bent down to trim a perfect leaf.

Kamla could still not look her daughter in the eye, without a pang.

It is a dark day, indeed, when mother and daughter heap insults, and call each other names. A day that is not easily forgotten.

They had rushed off to bury their shame – she, under her

68

blanket and her daughter, in the pages of her journal.

Now, months later they were still being cautious, like house kittens, new adoptees that circled each other, marking their territory, and inching closer daily.

Kamla had a sister who disappeared from their parents' home, at age twenty-two. Rumour had it, she eloped with the gardener's boy, a fate far worse than death, as far as her parents were concerned. She also had a brother they lost to the war in China, a tragedy that ran so deep, that Kamla did not dare excavate his memory for fear of turning into ashes herself.

Kamla's sister was four years older than her. Her parents never recovered from her betrayal and made their own and Kamla's life unbearable with their endless, stoic suffering.

And now, years later, she, Kamla had a daughter who resembled, in more ways than one, her runaway sister. The same dark colouring, Kamla thought, with a tightness in her chest, the same lack of discernment under a cladding of over-intelligence that gets you nowhere in a man's world.

Babuji tried without success to reason with his wife, "Women have way more options these days, Kamla! They can go anywhere, do whatever the heart desires, soar above the clouds, instead of tying their fate to a stranger."

Soar above the clouds indeed! As if they were not girls but Myna birds. Kamla wished she could drag Babuji back to earth from his useless notions. He was infecting their daughter with too much independence - study more. Travel more. Think more. Ishhhh!

No more! Kamla wanted to scream. She wanted for Sami, what she had for herself. A beautiful home. Comfort. Security. The thought that her daughter might share her sister's fate, terrified her. The fear settled in her bones and made her arthritic. It made her toes curl outwards and her gait unsteady. Kamla would not suffer another runaway. Could not spend her life yearning for the sweet relief of having her home.

Not in this lifetime, she vowed to herself.

Maya looked at her watch for the third time and vowed to out wait the man. It was 10.30 a.m. She'd been waiting 30 minutes. I bet, he's hoping I'll just go away, she thought, sourly.

She had wangled this interview after three relentless weeks of flirting, and she was not going to blow it just because he kept her waiting on a bench like a bloody underling. But isn't that the position she was applying for? An underling, a PA to the vice-chairman?

Well, one has to start somewhere, she thought, pragmatically.

Besides, it was her only way out of the time warp that was Kamla's world, where every moment, Maya sniffed, was like a teeny tiny needle sticking in the back of her neck.

The minutes ticked on. Maya pressed a middle finger on the side of her head, massaged it in a low circular motion. Almost an hour later, the receptionist, a woman much younger than Maya, sporting a red blazer and a permanent smirk, told her, 'He will see you now', jerking her chin toward his office. Maya stood up, smoothed her skirt, and walked in the direction she was pointed.

"Maya, sorry to keep you waiting, sit, relax, coffee? Coke?"

She accepted a Coke.

He rang for a peon. A small boy in a khaki uniform appeared out of nowhere.

"One Coke."

The boy disappeared.

"So, tell me, why do you want this job?" He drummed his

fingers on the desk like a very busy vice-chairman, making it clear the man who passed his hands over her bum more than once and slurred, he had this thing for older women, was not the same person seated across the table from her.

"I want to be around smart, intelligent people. The kind of men," she gestured lightly, including him with an almost imperceptible bow, "who make a difference. Have avant-garde ideas. Men who will put India on the same footing as other first world countries."

"I want to be part of the future, not the past, despite my great age," she smiled, risking a little self-deprecation.

He nodded thoughtfully. "But why do you think you are a suitable candidate for this specific job?"

Maya handed him her resume and ignoring the throbbing in her head, elaborated on her education, the degree from Columbia, her organizational skills. Finally, she did a little celebrity name dropping, thanks to the number of years she'd spent writing for tabloids in Kolkata, and reiterated she wanted to be surrounded by smart, effective men like you, Mr Batliwala.

"How is it you, a tabloid reporter, were able to get an interview with Mr Tata, in his home?" Batliwala held her resume but spoke to her breasts.

She shrugged. "Homework and persistence," she said. "I would do the same for you. Working for you would be such a learning opportunity!

He seemed genuinely impressed.

Although, of course, he would be. Stroke a lion's ego with your painted nails, then watch him purr like a pussy cat, Maya thought, even as she nodded at whatever he was saying, hand under her chin, fascinated.

One hour and forty-five minutes later she was escorted to HR. Another solid hour before she held a 2-year contract as executive assistant to the second-in-command of India's largest television network, in her hot little hands.

"So, see you this evening at the club? We must celebrate." The vice-chairman smiled, his lips parting like a bulldog, as he walked her back to the lobby. It was now past 2 p.m. Maya nodded, *the slug didn't even have the courtesy to offer me a sandwich*, gazed up at him with stars in her eyes.

The receptionist looked up from filing her nails. Maya watched with satisfaction as the woman's jaw dropped. She'd obviously seen the contract peeking out of her open bag.

Be careful you don't swallow a fly, Maya wanted to say. But again, she kept her counsel.

Her head still throbbed but it no longer bothered her. "Yes, we must celebrate." She scratched one teasing finger down his open-necked shirt. Blood entered Batliwala's corpora cavernosa and his veins compressed. His eyes fairly popped out of his head. The vice chairman's trousers, Maya noted with satisfaction, looked painfully tight.

"But not today." Maya moved towards the revolving doors. "Today, I have a daughter to present."

She was always fully present. Immersed in the business of life. And Babuji appreciated it. He really did. Especially, these days, with two additional, high-maintenance guests in the house.

The countless afternoons Kamla sacrificed - The naps, massages, daytime soaps she had to forego, so that she could shop, strategise, and spread the word like a gossip columnist about the girl's marketable attributes – her porcelain skin, her grey eyes, resplendent as the ocean at dusk, her Brahmin purity.

But why would a nineteen-year-old consent to being married in such an archaic fashion? Khushi should have been raised to believe in herself. To look beyond the periphery of the picket fence and find her passion. Instead ... he shook his head in bewilderment.

This beautiful girl, not that much older than Sami, (a shudder ran through Babuji's body) shined and polished daily like a piece of silver, then put on display before a group of strangers, to be appraised for her market value! And yet, in Khushi's eyes, he saw no conflict. Only a quiet excitement, an unspoken hope. He could not fathom it.

"It is what she wants, Sri!" Kamla told him for the hundredth time. "I am only doing what she begged me to."

"I cannot fathom it." Babuji lamented.

Harrumph! Kamla said in disgust and went into the kitchen for a final check.

Maya arrived almost at the same time as the guests and did not get a chance to take Kamla aside and apologize for being derelict, making a mental note, however, to thank her sister-in-law at a future date, perhaps with a box of sweets or a sari, for her selfless efforts.

How remarkably well she looks! Babuji thought and couldn't help wondering whether he had some small part to play in his sister's newfound happiness. He continued to try everything in his power to make her comfortable despite the fact that Kamla (women!), Babuji sighed, was upset he was not giving her the same dosage of care and solicitude he meted out to Maya.

Kamla, very much in her element, made sure to ask everyone to be seated and lowered her frame into a correspondingly adipose chair.

Khushi, fragrant, pulsating with blood and dreams and a lingering radiance (from many secret rituals), sat flanked by Babuji on her left and her mother on the right. Sami, closest to the hallway, kept a stern eye on the staff - they were given explicit instructions to behave like androids, not cough or smile too much, not walk into the room with jerky movements, but not stiff as sleepwalkers either, and unless asked a direct question, maintain a low profile. In other words, pretend they were deaf unless spoken to directly and mute when serving the guests (big baksheesh if they could manage the latter).

Cheetah seated casually on the first stair leading up to the second floor, made up a story on the spot, about Khushi, a creature of the spirit world, descending delicately upon earth, (purpose unknown) warding off evil suitors with mournful eyes and lush green wings on her shoulders.

The Mehtas, honoured guests, appeared decent enough. And the prospective groom (no one even thought to introduce him), looked self-satisfied – not devastatingly handsome, but not repulsive either, Sami thought.

Conversation flitted past Khushi, settled on one family member, drank deep from the cup of his/her wisdom, and moved on to the next. Maya intimidated the Mehtas with her wit and exuberance. Babuji impressed them with his judicious remarks. Kamla plied them between pauses, with sweet and salty snacks and in the midst of it all sat Khushi, tall and seemingly unruffled with her hands folded on her lap.

Sami tried to imagine them together, Khushi and the Mehta guy. Instead, to her horror, she saw Khushi standing before a mirror in a white slip, cupping one naked breast.

Change of scene! Change of scene! Sami shrieked (silently of course). Maybe she hit rewind in error, because Khushi was at it again, except this time, it was a man's hand, Mehta guy's hand fondling her breast and tweaking her nipple until it hardened like a bud. Desperately, Sami tried to focus on something else, anything else … stared at the mouth nearest to her, open and close voicelessly like a fish, but conversations, like gusts of wind, blew by or melded senselessly, until at last, one voice tore itself from the others. It was the Mehta guy asking her if she would pass the Pepsi, please. Sami looked at his mouth, looked up at his face, made eye contact, turned a deep shade of crimson, and flew to her room.

Hours later, Babuji knocked at her door.

"You didn't eat," he said.

"I'm not hungry," Sami said until she saw the paper plate heaped with all the things she loved. How does he always know?

"Babuji." She smiled.

"Eat," he said.

After she'd chewed the last morsel of kebab, swallowed the last bite of her chutney sandwich, and polished off the fruit cake, he said, "Your cousin is engaged. What do you think of that?"

"Ishhhh!" Said Sami, exactly like her mother, then laughed with merriment. Babuji looked at his daughter, how like yet thoroughly unlike she was all the women in his home, then threw his head back and laughed with her, until she held her sides, and tears streamed down his cheeks.

Much later, ensconced on his favourite chair, the door of his office determinedly shut, Babuji thought with exquisite relief - Sami will soar and sail above the clouds no matter what Kamla has to say. She will fly in the teeth of tradition. She will not abase herself for any man – not his daughter.

Twelve

Kamla, labouring to keep pace with her daughter, cursed her left knee, the bunions on her right foot, the pain in her lower back that throbbed with each step, cursed even the wind whistling nasally, picking up pollutants and scattering them with devilish pleasure all over her saree, her face, making her sneeze.

"Will you please slow down, Sami, do you want to kill me?"

"Still slower? We'll never get there on time!" Sami shot back, crossly.

Kamla bit her tongue. It wasn't often that Sami consented to go anywhere with her, least of all to the movies. If she, Kamla was to say something acerbic now, her daughter might deny her the pleasure of her company for a very long time. And Kamla could not have that. I should have worn flat sandals, she sighed mournfully and continued to pick her way through the congested mall, her eyes fixed firmly on her daughter's squared shoulders.

Abruptly, Sami came to a halt, pulled out a ticket from her purse and handed it to her mother.

"Here we are. You go sit down in the movie theatre now Amma, up those stairs and to the left... I need to... you know... got to the washroom."

"I'll wait here," Kamla started to say, then changed her mind when she was rudely elbowed by a bunch of excited teens.

Potato chips decorated her seat like confetti.

"Ishhhh!" A visibly annoyed Kamla, pulled out a tissue from her purse to clear the crumbs, letting them fall at her feet. Then she sat down, hands folded in front of her almost prayerfully and forced herself to relax in the darkened movie hall. Sami was still in the lavatory, probably waiting her turn in one of those snaking long lines, Kamla thought. She dozed off, confident her mental clock would wake her in time to stand for the national anthem.

Twenty-five minutes later, she stood for the anthem, looking blearily for Sami at each one of the exits. Should I worry, she wondered, when she saw her daughter hasten in from a side entrance. "Ooof! There you are."

"Yes. Disgusting toilets," Sami shuddered. "Let's just watch the movie."

Kamla watched the movie without really following it, playing unconsciously with the ends of her heavy braid, the dreamy expression in her eyes somehow accentuated by her still thick, curling lashes.

She looks almost happy! Thought Sami, startled. I wonder what she's dreaming about. Like most children, she rarely, if ever, gave her mother's internal life any consideration.

After all, Amma was not so much a person as an Akshaya Patra of creature comforts. Without her talent for endless giving, she would be what? A joke? A shapeless bundle of idiosyncrasies, more sound than fury? Sami grinned to herself, wickedly.

They actually made me and Cheetah! She shook her head and focused on the screen to erase the disturbing image of her parents, cohabiting (fully clothed of course) in the corner bedroom.

Kamla was thinking, she'd finally pulled it off! With speed, diplomacy, and efficiency she had found Khushi a boy. The Mehta chap would make a wonderful husband for Khushi. He was good-looking and wealthy and so educated! How fortunate for the girl!

She wondered if her sister-in-law would give her carte blanche for the wedding arrangements. After all, Maya was never home. Always so busy with her highfalutin friends, Kamla ignored the stab of jealousy, when would she make time for the thousand and one little details involved in throwing a wedding when they could barely get her to arrive on time for her daughter's engagement ceremony!

They will see! They will be so impressed with my abilities, thought Kamla, but of course when she said 'they' it was the discerning Babuji she hoped to impress, and to some extent, her overly critical Sami.

Well, at least she chose to be with me today, her Amma, instead of gadding about with Maya somewhere. There's that. Kamla sighed loud and long, making Sami give her a sidelong glare.

They were barely out of the movie hall when Sami had to go again.

"But Sami, can't you wait until we get home?"

"No. I have my period."

"You don't! You had your period two weeks ago."

"Shhh! Amma! Go out, get a coconut drink, and wait for me by the kiosk. You must be thinking of your lovely Khushi," Sami said scathingly.

And Kamla, riddled with doubt, went to wait for her daughter by the said kiosk.

When in doubt, don't! Khushi's father had once advised. This, from a man who spent his whole life doing exactly the opposite.

But the adage stuck – long after her father absconded for pleasures unknown – perhaps because her mind remained uncluttered by other bits of wisdom.

When the Mehta boy, or BK as he liked to be called - especially in the throes of passion - began making a weekly appearance at the Solanki residence, Khushi hoped her good-girl ensemble, that is, full-sleeves tunic, pants and scarf, and matt make-up would help tamp down both his lust and hers. But beneath this naïve hope lingered an opposite, fierier emotion. It was this emotion she stoked, when she waxed her legs and her thighs and all the parts he ought not to touch (as yet), and rubbed perfumed body lotion into her arms, her neck, and behind her knees, then lifted her hair in a top knot so that his breath might catch at the sight of her delicate nape, and cause him to kiss it, almost inadvertently, when he bent down to greet her.

Khushi, my *khushi* (happiness), he would whisper the moment they were alone. And she would blush and blush as if it was not a play on words she had been hearing for the past nineteen years.

"Let us sit in the drawing room," she would respond in a deliberately loud and boisterous voice as if tone deaf to the longing in his voice. There, within earshot of the maids, she played hostess, offering him more and more of the inevitable tea and samosas, until with the air of a flayed horse, he rose and left.

Once in her own bedroom, Khushi would tear off her clothes, as if on fire. I have to be good until the wedding, that's what is expected of me, of any respectable young woman. It's so unfair to be tormented in such a way! She'd sigh dramatically and press a damp towel to her neck.

<hr>

Maya sighed in a self-satisfied way, celebrating her well-earned freedom with a refreshing glass of vodka and tonic. Within only a matter of months, she had made herself indispensable to the vice chairman. Now he sat gazing at her with disturbing intensity, breathing noisily like a dog in heat.

"You should eat something. Not a good idea to drink on an empty stomach," Maya said lazily.

"Yeah, okay. Hey, Maya, I was thinking..."

"Oh, oh..." Maya's eyes danced. "Am I in trouble?"

He bared his teeth.

"I think you are being underutilized in that closet, creating itineraries and planning events. I think you should..."

"Mr Batliwala, fancy seeing you here!" Maya cursed under her breath as a rotund woman with shopping bags in both hands flashed her dimples and leaned forward for a kiss-kiss.

Introductions were made, precious minutes lost on pleasantries, the lady accepted, then refused, then accepted a drink, until it was time for her to leave. Batliwala looked at his watch and glanced at the drink Maya was still working on.

"Oh, don't worry about me, if you must go. I'll be fine."

"Yes. Okay. My apologies. We will talk, ya?"

You bet we will, she wanted to say, but merely nodded agreeably.

He hurried off to rendezvous with his wife. Maya knew he screwed his wife once a week. How could she forget? It was Maya who was asked with a wink and a leer, to order a bottle of wine and make sure it was fruity not floral tasting, for his quiet evening at home.

"Happy wife, happy life," he said, with a nauseating smirk every Friday, until she countered, "Doesn't take that much to make her happy, does it?" Then realized she'd gone too far when she saw the warning in his eyes. Lesson learned: lose the rapier wit if you want to win points with 'manly' men.

Maya nursed her drink, doing her best to not jump ahead and imagine a future outside the closet that served as her office.

PR executive? Company ambassador? She wiped the corner of her lips in disgust. I'm positively drooling, for god's sake! It was as she was putting down her napkin that she caught sight of Sami, hanging outside the restaurant.

Their eyes met, and Sami hastened to meet her, a shy smile on her face.

"What are you doing here, my girl?" Maya smiled back warmly.

"I actually came to see you. I saw you on my way to the pharmacy next door." She pointed her chin at the unscreened window.

Maya wasn't buying her explanation, there were several pharmacies in Sami's neighbourhood, why come this far? But she held her tongue.

"Ah! Now you've seen me. Sit." She said and waited until Sami sat hesitatingly down.

"Auntie, I was wondering, could you help me get a dress?"

Maya reached for her purse.

"No ... no I have cash." Sami coloured.

"I mean pick a dress. For a party, you see. Khushi always dresses beautifully, but I mean, my style ... I'm not certain."

"Of course, dear. Let's pick something more you. Quietly sexy, pert without looking like a Bollywood star."

Sami grinned happily. "Is that how you see me?"

"That is how you see yourself." And added, "I like it."

A radiant Sami leaned forward and kissed Maya on the cheek, then sat back stunned. She was. rarely, if ever, overtly affectionate.

Maya too seemed happily surprised.

Kamla happily surprised to be asked, sat in a rare moment of quietude beside her husband.

A wooden bed converted cleverly into a porch swing, hung from a festive, Jaipuri awning. The Judge and his wife took turns pushing on the concrete floor with the heel of one foot, making their seat rock gently as a cradle. A solitary star stood witness in the evening sky.

"Khushi will be married, this time next year. I did not say it before, but you were very generous with your time and effort on my niece's behalf," The judge said, magnanimously.

Kamla blushed prettily.

"Sri," she said softly. He looked up pleased. It wasn't often his wife called him by name, preferring the respectful *Aap* or *Ji* as coached by her parents.

"Yes." He took her hand in his own.

"Sami seems quite distracted these days," Kamla steered the conversation away from herself.

"Her grades are fine."

"Oyeee!" Kamla emitted. "It is important to be a well-rounded person. To develop other talents, skills, a pleasant attitude, to be a success in life. Grades are not everything." She held her breath waiting to be chastised.

But Babuji was looking at her thoughtfully, with something akin to respect.

"I agree, Kamla."

She coloured. Perhaps she thought he was being patronizing.

"Your opinion means so much to me. Some days ... you see ... I feel quite pointless." Kamla averted her head.

Then Babuji did something she never allowed, outside the privacy of their bedroom. He leaned forward and kissed her hand.

"Kamla. I know. I know what I mean to you. I just wish I could make you understand, what you mean to me."

Kamla withdrew her hands in alarm. "Ishhhh! How can you ... the maid ... Radha ..." she muttered. Babuji smiled, and retreated to his corner.

Radha, the maid was so happy she wished she could spread her feathers like a peacock and dance in the rain. Every muscle in her face twitched with emotion, every thought turned into song.

"Amma! Babuji! Amma!" She waltzed into the house, her bare feet thudding irrepressibly on the hallway floor.

"Radha, how dare you ..."

"Amma! We got it. The government is giving us a solid apartment, with walls, floors, a ceiling!"

Radha, the maid, spread her arms outward and upward, ready to take wing.

"Are you sure?" Babuji hearing the commotion came out in time to witness his maid's exultation.

"Where are the papers?"

Radha whipped out the paper carefully folded and tucked tightly in her waistband, signed with her thumbprint – she was quite illiterate – and presented it to Babuji as if it was her heart she was letting him cradle.

Babuji read the agreement carefully, taking a full thirty seconds, then smiled. "Yes. You have it. Will you not miss your village?"

"A village without electricity and no running water? They are welcome to my land. I will have a *pukka* home, like a *pukka* lady," as God is my witness, she almost said.

"Where are they building these apartments?" Kamla asked after a decent pause. She would have to find a new Radha if this one moved away.

"Only forty minutes from here, in Goregaon. Far, far closer to you than my village home in *Palghar*!" Radha grinned in triumph.

"Radha!"

"Yes, Amma."

"Here. Take this." Amma gave her a handful of notes, eager to participate in the maid's happiness and perhaps even get a little credit for it.

"You can use the money to fill up your new home. A gas stove. Some utensils, yes?"

"Yes! A *pukka* home. With on/off switches. A latrine. Utensils." Radha, the maid, laughed shrilly then burst into tears.

Thirteen

Khushi burst into tears at the news.

"But what will I do for two weeks... without you?"

"Really Khushi, you must be mature about this," BK said, tenderly.

"There is us. And there is work. I cannot very well tell my boss I won't travel because my fiancé will miss me."

"I wish I was your boss," she hiccupped between tears.

"You want to be my boss? What will you have me do?" He moved dangerously close, backing her into a wall.

Khushi looked as if she was going to pass out, whether from fear or a surfeit of desire, it was unclear.

There was a sound. He let go.

"Oh, Sami, it's you. I thought it was ... someone else" Khushi said, trying to feign nonchalance.

"Oh Khushi, it's you, I thought it was the washerwoman," Sami countered, nodding at the Mehta guy, and taking the stairs two at a time.

Sami dropped her book bag tiredly. She had math homework, and a Nature versus Nurture essay to tackle. And she still did not have a dress for the end-of-school year party.

She wondered if auntie Maya would make time to take her shopping, as promised. Auntie Maya was generous but unlike Amma, put herself both first, and second, and everybody else a distant third. Still. She was so elegant, so fantastic, Sami thought wistfully.

There was a knock.

"Come in."

It was Khushi.

"Sami, I hope we didn't embarrass you earlier." Khushi blushed.

"We? Oh, you mean you and the Mehta guy, I mean, your fiancé. No. Why would I be embarrassed?"

"He was trying to comfort me, you see," Khushi said softly.

"Oh. I didn't realize you needed comforting." Sami looked at her cousin curiously.

"Well, he can't see me for a bit. Going away on work." Khushi looked as if she was about to cry.

A quiver of schadenfreude shot through Sami, taking her by surprise. Sami did not like her cousin. Everybody, including Babuji, treated her like Dresden china, so afraid she would shatter if one so much as raised a voice in her vicinity. She was way too fair, way too feminine, way too saccharine, making her, Sami, feel like a bull in a china shop. But she wasn't envious of her cousin. Was she? Even Babuji agreed, although not in so many words, that the girl had no mettle, was rather vacuous.

"But he will be back, won't he?" Sami said, trying to infuse kindness into her words.

"Yes. But what will I do in the meantime?"

"Really, Khushi, can't you entertain yourself? He is not your boy doll!"

Khushi whimpered like a startled bunny, and scuttled out of the room, shutting the door gently behind her.

Barely had the door closed, then it opened again. It was Amma.

"Sami, you could be kinder to your cousin! She is sad. You could ..."

"Amma! Leave me alone. Why must you always barge in? And why is she coming to me with her love problems, anyway? I can't help her. Am I her age?"

Amma about to say something stopped in her tracks. Then she nodded thoughtfully, as if digesting a new piece of information.

"That's right. You are not, are you? Sometimes we forget. There is a maturity about you Sami, that Khushi, at nineteen, does not seem to possess."

She says 'maturity' like I have an extra bloody nipple, Sami thought.

"I'm sorry. I will talk to Khushi," Amma finished, pacifically.

Of course, it would be too much to expect for Amma to ever leave, having said her piece. She continued to hang around.

"Still, she's here in a new city, alone and friendless. How would you feel, Sami, in her situation?"

"I would embrace my anonymity with open arms. I would rise at the crack of dawn, thumb down a rickshaw and discover the city from end to end with my Kodak camera. I would sniff out our fantastic street foods and make use of our many resources – the library, the club, the beaches, the shops, the ..."

But Amma had left the room. Grinning evilly, Sami went to the door, stood on her toes, and slid the latch in place.

Despite her heels, Maya had to stand on her toes and lean over from the balcony of Nirvana apartments in Breach Candy, to see just how far one could fall. She shuddered and turned around to face the realtor.

"Rather high up, aren't we? What if the elevator doesn't work? I will have to trudge up, what, 37 floors?"

"Don't worry. No creaky elevators here," said the realtor. "This is a brand-new building. They are still putting the finishing touches on the mural in the lounge, in case you didn't notice. And, I should have pointed out, there are three lifts. Two for home owners and one for the staff." Like all International students, the realtor switched often between American and British English.

"Plus, the builder has pre-emptively made provisions for emergency generators," she added, a tad smugly.

From inside came the sound of a toilet being flushed. Both women frowned with distaste. The realtor, a Parsee woman almost as tall and elegant as Maya but settled into a permanent pear shape, stroked her silk scarf, unconsciously.

"Ah, here's Percy, now. What do you think, should we let her have the apartment?" She prodded him with a knuckle, playfully.

Maya bristled. The assumption that it was up to Percy to decide for her was not very flattering. But to be fair, the realtor was Batliwala's contact. It was almost certain he had given her the impression they were lovers looking for a cosy little nook for their clandestine affair.

She turned her back on the realtor, and asked pointedly, "Can we discuss this in private please, Mr Batliwala?"

"Oh, sorry. Of course. I have a few calls to make. I will be in the other room." The realtor strode off with a genial smile in their direction.

"What do you think?" He asked, placatingly.

"Do I get a house rent allowance? Now that I'm a publicity manager?"

"I thought you got one already."

"I saw a laughable number on my last paycheck. I cannot afford to rent a mousetrap, leave alone this flat, based on what I saw."

"I don't know if I can justify a larger allowance, Maya."

"Then why bother bringing me here?" Maya said, a trifle sharply.

"It will save me an hour and a half of commuting time." She softened her tone.

"And, I wouldn't have to leave the office before rush hour every evening. Now, this living area," she gesticulated, "I just realized, is perfect for your meetings with out-of-town visitors. So centrally located! Khushi might be happier here as well," she added, almost as an afterthought, then stopped. Don't overkill. She held her breath.

Batliwala nodded thoughtfully. "All right."

Maya, gripped with conflicting emotions, exhaled.

"Thank you, Percy." It did not escape his notice that she called him by name, and in quite an intimate tone. He felt a familiar flutter.

"But do you really think you want to displace your daughter one more time? Why not let her stay with this uncle and aunt who appear to care for her so deeply, and continue her education at the local university until next year when she marries?"

Maya looked at him, stung. The very thought had occurred to her, of course, but she did not care to have her guilty daydream voiced by an outsider.

"And, it will be easier for me, for business reasons, to keep our appointments without an impressionable young girl hanging about." The air crackled with the unsaid.

"Possibly. I have to speak with my brother," Maya shrugged. "Other than that, we are clear, the company will pay my rent?"

"The company will give you a very decent allowance, that will help towards the rent," he clarified, then put out his hand.

Maya took his hand. With his other hand, he brushed off a wayward hair sticking damply to her generous chest. Then with the flick of his middle finger, he released a button and found her soft spot. His glasses, she noted, were quite fogged.

From the darkened hallway the realtor watched, eyes gleaming with triumph.

The whites of his eyes gleaming, Cheetah raced home with his news.

"Oy, have you been rolling in mud, Cheetah, you little monkey?" Sami shouted from her balcony.

Cheetah looked up, grinning. "Am I a cheetah, or a monkey?"

"You are a cheetah-monkey. I bet you won. Did you?"

Cheetah nodded vigorously, beaming from ear to ear.

"Come on up!" Sami ordered.

He disappeared through the front door and appeared at her side in a blink.

"I'm going to squeeze you to death," she warned, pretending to lunge.

Cheetah took a step forward, then stopped. "It will ruin your dress."

Sami looked down at her dress. Auntie Maya had come through and taken her shopping. The party was the next day, but she couldn't resist trying the dress on one more time, in front of the mirror. Both the shop girl and auntie Maya thought she looked, "like a vision in azure."

"Stay with this colour Sami. You look beautiful. And so grown-up!" Auntie Maya looked almost shocked.

Cheetah was looking at her from under hooded eyes, shyly. Sami pulled her dress down, a little self-consciously.

"Oh, it's for the party tomorrow. Do you like it?"

He nodded. "You look pretty."

"Not as pretty as Khushi, though, ha?" She teased.

Cheetah stood stock still. What to say? What to do? "You are better than Khushi. I mean ... more fun."

Sami nodded. She was still smiling, but her eyes looked far away. A little sad.

"I meant ... more ... uh ... interesting."

Sami picked up a bath robe and wrapped it tightly around herself. "Be prepared to get crushed, track-champion cheetah-monkey." She opened her arms and let him nestle in her musky warmth.

Kamla stirred, stretched and opened her arms to a new dawn. Outside her window, the water sprinkler wooed the wilting bushes with ardour. Inside, the aroma of medium roast arabica coffee filled her like body heat. Kamla breathed in the sounds and smells and was filled with a delicious sense of well-being.

I think I'll make Sri's favourite pudding, she smiled. Where is that lazy Radha?

Radha, the maid, was slow to rise. She had been kept up most of the night by her husband. He had allowed himself to be lured into Raju's Best Bar and spent a full week's paycheck on a bottle of illicit cashew liquor with strong undertones of kerosene oil.

Filled with bonhomie, he threaded his way home, where alas, he felt compelled to mark his territory in every corner of the house like a one-testicle cur. An hour later he had to get up again, this time to heave and hurl a disgusting yellow stream from his other orifice, his mouth.

It was 3.30 a.m. before Radha felt comfortable he would live, and with infinite disgust, she closed her eyes.

Having cleaned her entire hutment with industrial strength peroxide, now running late for work, she pushed her way into the local train, congested even at that godforsaken hour. Vagrants, shapeless as heaped litter, pressed against each other or squatted wherever they could find a square inch, head between their knees.

A hawker thrust a potato roll under her nose.

"No." Radha, the maid, shuddered. She would wait until she was in the sparkling white Solanki kitchen, make herself some buttered toast and wash it down with a strong cup of coffee in their best china cup when the cook's back was turned. I deserve it, she thought. It was a phrase she'd picked up from Maya madam. Radha quite liked the sound of it.

About to cross the street to her place of work, she was almost knocked down by a motorbike. Of course, the rider did not stop. Why would he? She was a shoeless servant. He was a big shot Sahib on wheels!

But even as she jumped back in terror, she recognized that Mehta boy. Why, he's supposed to be out of town! That's why Miss Khushi is moping around.

She wondered if she should mention it in passing to Kamla. Perhaps, when I learn more, she decided. Something told her, there was more.

For the first time in fourteen hours, Radha, the maid, smiled, albeit a malicious smile.

Just you wait, Bali Sahib, Karma is about to bite you in the butt, she might have said. But not being versed with the ways of karma, she merely sneered and thought *you will get yours, mother f******. I will see to it. Then she filled her mouth with phlegm and flung her contempt onto the street.

Fourteen

Bali Mehta, BK to his paramours, took a last bite of his apple and flung the core onto the street. A stray dog ran between two cars, to retrieve his treasure.

"You should put it in the trash," his nephew frowned.

"Do you see a trash can anywhere? The whole city is a dump." Bali sniggered. "Let's go." He strode ahead of Bobby. "Get it over with."

Young Bobby sighed inwardly. Bali had promised him a pair of distressed Levi's jeans if he accompanied him to his prospective in-laws' place. And he, in a moment of weakness, had agreed.

Bali rang the doorbell. A brief wait, the sound of bare feet slapping against the floor and then the door opened.

"Mehta sahib," Radha stared, with studied insolence.

"Hello Radha, nice saree," Bali stared openly at her cleavage.

Radha, not to be outdone in the impertinence department, undid her *Pallu* with one flick to reveal two perfect breasts gift-wrapped in a loosely knotted, braless blouse. Next, with the air of a woman who has all the time in the world, she pushed the trailing fabric into her waistband, letting him enjoy her goodie bag more fully, including the divine inverted parenthesis that was her waist and her coffee-coloured belly button.

"Are you here for Miss Khushi? Or?" She all but winked.

"Yes. And Miss Sami, if she's home. I want to introduce my nephew to the family." He said, his eyes still licking her many luscious parts.

Bali took one step to the left to reveal an open-mouthed Bobby.

"Mmm." Radha gestured to the living room and went to notify Kamla, swaying her hips, like the siren that she was.

From inside came the sound of Kamla, scolding. "Why are you exposing your breasts in that shameless fashion? Cover yourself."

"Sorry, Amma. I'm so hot."

Then the sound of feet thumping down the stairs. It was Sami.

She saw BK first, then the uncomfortable looking boy in khakis. "Ho ho! Two for the price of one." She tittered.

Poor Kamla, still discomfited by Radha's lewd display of flesh, huffing in to greet the visitors, had the misfortune of hearing her daughter's crass remark.

"Sami!" Her eyes bulged. Young Bobby turned scarlet and even Bali passed a hand across his face.

"Just joking, Amma, you have no sense of humour." Sami stamped her feet.

"Go back upstairs and stay in your room. Send your cousin down, instead. Ah! Here she is." Amma patted a chair and purred like a kitten with a saucer of milk, "Khushi, come join us. You look beautiful!"

Sami flushed. Bali smiled in a conciliatory fashion.

"Oh. You should stay, Sami. It's okay, Auntie. I thought it would be nice for all of us to be friends. This is my nephew, Bobby." Bali smiled his best smile.

"Harrumph. Okay." Then pointing her chin at Sami, she said,

"You! Don't sit too long. And don't talk. Don't humour. Don't ..." Amma ran out of don'ts.

"Yes, Amma." Sami conceded meekly. Amma went back into the kitchen, with a warning glance at her brazen daughter. For a few seconds, the entire group looked whipped.

"Even her back looks affronted," Sami finally whispered, then began giggling hysterically. And in spite of themselves, the others followed suit.

Babuji walked towards his study and Kamla followed suit. He looked at his wife perturbed. This was his private domain. His inner sanctum. Babuji never merely entered his study. Slowing his breath, relaxing with each step, he floated into a gloriously meditative state.

And Kamla was well aware of the way he felt. Yet here she was, crowding his space, shattering his equilibrium like a carpet salesman barging into a Himalayan retreat.

"Can I help you, Kamla?" He asked with a pained expression.

"Help me? Why start now?" Clearly, his wife was in a contentious mood.

Babuji merely looked at her. He dared not sigh.

"It's Bali. He's always here. Now a book for Khushi, now a CD for Khushi. How long will this go on? Why can't he set a date for the wedding?" She glared at Babuji malevolently as if it was all his fault.

"Have you spoken to his parents?"

"You are so clever. Of course, I have. They said it is up to their son. Up to their son! Ishhhh! What an irresponsible thing to say." Kamla held both hands to the heavens asking the gods to attest.

"Well, Kamla," he added hesitantly, "My dear. Surely, we can leave Khushi to her own fate now? I mean, let Khushi and her mother decide ..."

"Maya! You want to leave Khushi's fate in Maya's hands? Your sister cannot handle her own unsavoury fate." The implication of this remark seared Babuji, making him cringe and pale.

Kamla seeing his pain, shut up at once. She wondered if it would help to touch him.

The railway-station style clock above Babuji's desk ticked on mutedly.

"I have to see to their snacks," Kamla finally muttered and started to leave.

"Kamla. Do you remember how it was, when we were first engaged? I know it was for a short time, and it has been many years, but do you remember?" Babuji sounded faraway, pensive.

"Yes. I surely do."

"We rarely got to talk. I was so happy just to see you, if only for a few moments, silently moving from one room to another, as I sat making small talk with your aunts, your grandmother. Just to know you were there, somewhere in the vicinity, thinking of me too perhaps, it made me supremely happy. I wrote poems, whole verses on the way your feet rested in their golden juttis, the one stray curl under your ears ... silly, immature stuff, but surely the sentiment was original for me."

Kamla stared at him. Unbeknownst to her, she had taken on his exact expression – pensive, nostalgic, sad.

"What is your point, Sri?" She whispered.

"Let them be. Soon Khushi will be married. Engross herself with the art of making samosas, mending clothes, rearing children. For now, let them exchange glances, CDs. Let them be for a while."

"But what if something inappropriate ..."

"No. Not with Khushi. Nothing will happen."

"Okay then. Okay." Kamla, suddenly self-conscious, left the room.

"**Y**es. I will see you in a few minutes. Okay then. Okay. Bye."

"Who's that, Sami?"

"Oh, no one."

"Sami! You are blushing. Who is it?"

"Honestly, Khushi. If you must know, that was Bobby Mehta. He asked me to go out for a walk with him. Get some ice cream."

"You can't. Auntie won't like it!"

"I can't have ice cream?"

"You know what I mean. You can't go alone, with a boy."

"What century are we in?" Sami glared at her cousin.

Then, as if struck by inspiration, she said, "Hey, why don't you call Bali as well? The two of you can chaperone the two of us."

"I can't."

"Come on, Khushi, at least play at Little Women before you get to the Good Wives bit."

Khushi knew her cousin was probably alluding to some tiresome fictional characters, decided it was easier to simply sigh and nod assent rather than ask her to explain.

"Okay. Let me change into something nicer."

"Change into something nicer, for ice cream! Jeez! Okay! I will have my Bobby call your Bali to say we'll be there." Sami grinned.

Khushi pinked a little, not sure whether Sami was being funny, in which case she ought to laugh, or maliciously using the possessive pronoun, when referring to Bali. Pretending to cough, she went off to get changed.

Khushi desperately wanted to see her fiancé, but she much preferred that he called her. Not the other way around. She wasn't exactly thrilled to be out with Sami either. All her boisterous talk was way too distracting. Last week, huddled with Bobby and Sami in the living room, Bali had scarcely noticed her baby pink lip gloss and didn't seem to care that she'd taken the time to let loose her braids, and brush her hair to a sheen before she joined them. To be fair, auntie Kamla did not make it easy for the young lovers either, always hovering over them with platters of food.

Bobby, at least, could not stop gawking at her, Khushi thought with a smile. It was weird. The boy didn't appear interested in Sami, yet here he was asking her cousin out. Yeah, it must be her wit. Sami did have a way with words ...

"Hurry up! Or I'm leaving!" Sami broke into her reverie.

Khushi winced. "Must you be so loud, Sami?"

"Yes, I must."

She hurried down, but not before dipping a finger in her favourite perfume bottle and dotting it behind each shell-like ear.

Radha, the maid, dotting attar behind each ear, performed her latest Bollywood number for the watchman.

"How does this move look? Am I doing it well?" She was leaning forward doing a shimmy.

"Don't jerk your shoulders so much. You look like a horse having a seizure."

Radha giggled. She scarcely ever took offence at his little insults.

Moderately pleased though she was with her current placement, sometimes Radha was still bitten by the acting bug. Years ago, clad in a crop top and gauze skirt – she auditioned for every pissant Producer in show business. When the last scrap of rice in her copper pot and the last coin tucked away in her blouse, somehow disappeared into the pocket of a greasy-haired Agent, she decided on a new career path.

These days, 'Item girls' or strip club dancers, were all the rage – and Radha, certain she had the moves down to a science, was gyrating for her sometimes lover.

"How about this ... or this?" She pushed out one hip, one hand on her waist, the other behind her head.

"Old," said the watchman. "You are not putting enough oomph into it. Imagine a suited-booted sahib, smacking his lips. He wants class but he also wants to do you from the back. He wants to get in your pants, but he wants to make you work for it. Pretend, there's no one like him. He's a hero. The man of your dreams. Then do your dance. And, I promise you we'll soon be rolling on this very bed, in a shit load of cash."

"If I ever get a sahib to leave me a shitload of cash, why would I roll around on this bed?" Radha sneered, then made a grab for his member when he smote his chest, pretending to look stricken.

When they were done fooling around, she stuck her neck out of the watchman's shanty to catch some air. It was then that she saw the Mehta boy leave from the Solankis' front door. Something about the way he kept looking over his shoulder, gave her pause.

What is he up to?

Almost without thinking, she shrugged into her sari blouse, and without so much as a goodbye nod to the watchman, slunk out the door. Once on the street, making sure to cover her head so that she looked like any featureless servant crushing dirt under her callused feet, she followed the furtive Bali.

Discoloured paper festoons followed Atal like furtive ghosts. Some latched on to his foot so that he had to bend down and wrench the damn things off.

"Ugh! Like water snakes. What are we doing here? Why don't we just go home!"

"Don't be a sissy, Atal! Look. They are immersing another Ganesh in the ocean. Let's go watch."

Atal looked up at the sky. Rain clouds hovered ominously low threatening to swallow the rising waves, him and all his friends included. Just a few hundred yards from him, a crowd as thick as jungle trees chanting, *Ganpati Bappa Morya* ... surrounded an almost 12-foot clay idol, ready for immersion.

"I've seen it before. I'm going." Atal looked back, hoping his friends would fall in line. They didn't. Of course, he couldn't go home without them. For one thing, he did not know the bus number or the exact location of the stop, other than the fact that it was somewhere behind the taxi stand. But which taxi stand? What if there was more than one? They all looked the same. And he wasn't really certain where to get off either, even if he got on the right bus, he thought ashamedly. It was really unfair that Babuji didn't allow him to take public transport. Now, all his friends called him a ninny or a sissy.

Feeling rather sorry for himself, lost in thought, Atal walked for quite a while, then looked up suddenly, startled by the absence of sound. Both the body of water and the sea of humanity seemed to him sequestered behind a thicket of trees. The clouds lowered to the ground, scooped him up like a soft-boiled egg. He disappeared into a woolly greyness then emerged alongside a line of rustic cabins, hoping the familiar sight of slate and pine would shake off the sudden heaviness he felt.

The cabins had wide, curtainless windows and sloping roofs

designed purposefully to look like shanties but with clever, luxurious touches – brick patios, manicured bushes and solar lamps.

Atal thought he heard music and walked toward the sound. Was he imagining it or did the music decrescendo with each step? Soon it sighed off completely and by the time he got to the window of the cabin the silence was complete. He peered within.

Confusion, fear, and shock shot through Atal in equal parts.

Leave! He thought. Now!

Except he found himself rooted to the spot. At what he saw. What he could never unsee.

Hours later, or perhaps it was just moments, when the flutter in his chest, like a bird gone mad, quelled a little, Atal bent down, rolled up his jeans and shook each foot with his hands as if shaking a recalcitrant child. The numbness receded. Then he ran.

Fifteen

Skirting the sidewalk, ponytail bouncing behind her, Khushi ran for the No. 83 bus. Luckily for her, there was no oncoming traffic, because she was literally in the centre of the road.

Years ago, on her way to school, Khushi had once stepped on a bird. She remembered it well. She had lifted her feet and looked furtively about her, feeling responsible, although it was obvious the injury she'd caused the bird was only one of many, seeing how it lay there, quite still, except for its terrorized heart rising and falling in a last hurrah.

How was she to know, there was a Robin heaving its last breaths out on the sidewalk that was swept daily, sometimes twice a day, by the fastidious Parsee lady, next door? Khushi, bent down, gathered the wee creature and stuffed it in the pocket of her school overcoat, with one angry motion.

When she emptied her pockets, later that evening, she found the bird quite dead and frankly repelling. Unrecognisable bird bits poked out of the lining of her pocket, making her nauseous. Khushi trashed the bird, overcoat and all, without ceremony, in the nearest bin and never really thought about it again. Until recently.

Now, on particularly humid days, she could still smell the bird on her sneakers, feel the crunch of a broken wing under her heels. Which is why she began avoiding the sidewalk.

The No. 83 bus would take her to the train station. From there she intended to take the express train to Church Gate, where Maya would have a car and driver waiting for her.

"Let's do lunch," Maya had said, then added, "it's been a while, baby," in an effort to be loving.

As always, Khushi dressed with care, picking a starched white tunic and white pants for her luncheon. She wore no jewellery or scarf, choosing, instead, to accentuate her exfoliated (honey and brown sugar) pout with a startling shade of crimson. She knew she would have the desired effect – make her mother's eyes burn with envy.

The bus juddered to a stop. Khushi climbed in, saw an empty seat, or occupied a seat vacated for her by some sap she barely glanced at.

I've met Bali only three times, this entire month, she thought. In the past, that would have made her weep openly, unashamedly. Now she stuffed away her pain, much as she had stuffed the dead Robin in her overcoat, to be examined and nursed in private.

A flock of girls moved aside so that Khushi could get ahead of them in line. It was not her fault the world was full of saps, paying homage to her light skin, her pretty moue. She gravitated to the ticket counter, bought a two-way ticket, and made her way to the train.

A woman pressed her thighs together and angled her legs to the right to make room for Khushi.

She adjusted her body to fit into the freed space and nodded her thanks without making eye contact.

Khushi wrinkled her nose, buried it in a towelette moist with cologne and looked out the dismal window. The squalor long settled in the capillaries of the railway sank into her skin and spread equitably among the passengers.

Outside, there was nothing to see. There was a fixity to the landscape that held her eyes and made her head spin.

The spew of industry, the bloat of deprivation, the spit of disease, chug ... chug ... chug ... industry, deprivation, disease. No getting away from the nonstop bleakness. Nauseated, Khushi drew her eyes away from the window and looked sidelong at the commuters instead.

Eyes, black or brown, noses, short or blunt, ears, small or elephantine. All different and all the same. And behind those eyes, thought Khushi, now overcome with a sense of panic, that familiar, hollowed out hunger. The weary longing for someone or something just within reach, never quite attainable. How am I any different from any of these people, despite my smooth skin, and my red lips and my thick hair? We are all travelling with our two-way tickets. First, hoping to get away from it all, then eager to return. What is the point? The train roared and shuddered, farted effluvia. Her nausea grew exponentially.

If I were to simply throw myself ...

Where was Khushi going with this train of thought? Pointless to conjecture, because just then, the train arrived at platform number three and all passengers were advised to collect their personal belongings and mind their footing as they got off.

Suffice it to say, that Khushi, at age nineteen, was having an existential crisis (without quite knowing what that meant) en route to Church Gate Station.

Of course, it's entirely possible (and has been known to happen) that a concoction of fug and fust adhered to her skin like cling wrap seeped in gradually, replaced the oxygen in her bloodstream with mood-altering molecules, and brought her down with a crash.

Nothing would bring Maya down to a restaurant in the

causeway but a lunch date with her daughter. The whole strip was too harried, teeming with models, executives, small-time photographers with unkempt hair and ill-fitting garments, flaunting an inverse snobbery in a distasteful way. She had chosen Paradise, an informal hole in the wall with benches instead of chairs, lunch specials scribbled on a chalkboard and small plates. A not unpleasant smell of onion rings and hamburgers pervaded the air.

Hopefully, my clothes won't reek of incinerated cow, for the 3 pm meeting, she grimaced.

Khushi disliked large platters of food bursting at the seams like dissatisfied housewives. She also disliked buffet lines – all those cauldrons of orangey gravy rubbing against each other, shining with oil – enough to make you lose your appetite for food altogether. At least, I know her taste in cuisine, if nothing else, Maya told herself wryly, as she checked her make up in the mirror of her powder case. She closed the case, with a snap just as Khushi made her way to the table, her forehead glistening, her smile not quite reaching her eyes.

"Mama."

"Hello, Sweetie, come. Sit. Happy Birthday!"

A sap ran to pull a chair for Khushi. She sat down. Patted her forehead with the ends of her kerchief.

"You look lovely. How is everything going for you?"

"It's going. I like your hair like this. Up. Did you order, already?"

"No. I thought you could decide for both of us. I'm not that hungry. And, oh, here." Maya slid a little velvet jewellery box, without an accompanying card, across the table.

Khushi accepted the gift politely, guessing by the size of the box, it held earrings and placed it carefully in her purse. Then she ordered a tandoori chicken sandwich and tomato soup for herself. A chicken salad and coffee for her mother.

"Aren't you going to get a drink?" Maya asked.

"Can I have a beer?"

"I guess so, now that you are an old lady," Maya smiled, not trying to hide her surprise. Khushi, with one finger, motioned the waiter, to return. He tacked on the beer to her order, bending at the waist like a vassal, panicked and excited as a schoolboy.

They ate their meal quietly for a while. Maya found her chicken salad surprisingly good and decided she was a little hungry after all. The restaurant was filling up and the ambient noise made it impossible to make real conversation. Khushi, Maya noted, was merely picking at her meal.

"You don't like your sandwich?"

"It's good. I'm eating." Khushi took another bite and stared at her mother, making Maya raise her eyebrows in silent question.

"You decided to move away, just like Daddy."

Maya started to say something, but her daughter flicked her hand. "It is fine. Really. I'm old enough now, to do without either of you, and auntie Kamla is ..." she hesitated, "treats me well. I was wondering, though, if you are happy now that you are so independent?"

Maya stared at her daughter, dumbfounded.

Beneath the show of bravado and lurking resentment, was it possible Khushi was genuinely concerned about her mother's welfare? But since when was her daughter given to introspection? Maya tried to imagine the girl, rising that same morning, picking a crimson shade of lipstick, drawing the tube in a cupid's bow just a little above the lip line, pressing her full lips together then reapplying colour to make it hold. And then what? She looks into the mirror and wonders whether the mother who left her in Babuji's care without a sigh or a tear, was happy? Not bloody likely!

Maya decided to answer a question with one of her own.

"I'm happy enough. I'm a realist Khushi. I know this is as good as it gets for someone in my situation. But something else is on your mind, other than my welfare. Tell me, have you seen Bali, lately?"

Khushi straightened her back and dropped her spoon on the plate, making it squeak. "Not everything is about Bali, Mama," she said. Then burst into helpless tears.

It was a while before Khushi regained her composure. Maya did little more than take her daughter's hand and clasp it in both of her own. It seemed to be working. Taking deep breaths, Khushi smiled tentatively at last, a dewy wetness lingering on her overwrought lashes, and Maya, despite her consternation, could not help thinking Gawd, how can one look so beautiful despite those puffy eyes! Now, if only ...

But before she could follow that train of thought, her little girl, in a voice still shaky with emotion, made an announcement that filled her mother's heart with hope.

Radha, the maid missed being a little girl, quite literally. Her birth, she was told, with great hilarity, by a village elder, created one hell of a stir outside the village latrine, a single unit built with great fanfare by Congress just before elections.

As she squatted on the floor level WC, apparently the infant Radha, fell out of her mother's womb and had to be scooped out of the chamber pot caked with communal excrement. Her mother, not at all put out, gathered the gooey amalgam of flesh, blood and vernix into her arms and with a brisk swipe of her sari *pallu* muttered, "Get used to the stink little one, this is your life."

"Did the village women come to my mother's help when she screamed during labour?" Radha interrupted the woman.

"Oh, they probably thought she was constipated and those sounds they heard before she pushed you out, was just your mother straining to push out a piece of turd!" The crone smacked her toothless gums and hit her thigh in merriment.

"After she composed herself," she continued, "swaddling you as best as she could, with the less filthy parts of her *pallu* and ignoring all the harrumphs and taunts from the women waiting in line: the time some people took to shit as if they were memsahibs, your mother went into her hutment to prepare dinner."

At age two, Radha, awaiting her dinner, sat cross-legged on the floor by the stove. In the midst of slapping flatbread onto the *tawa* her mother suddenly froze.

Her pupils climbed into the back of her head, and she began rocking and muttering like one possessed. A horrified Radha watched the flame from the paraffin stove cackle and rise, her bread turn to ash, and black smoke tongue its way toward her throat.

"Aai!" She whimpered. It was how she addressed her mother.

"Aai!" She cried again, covering her ears with her hands as her mother responded with screams.

At some point, the smoke cleared, and Aai appeared in a cloud of soot rocking in her arms, a newly laid infant, no bigger than a rodent and just as black, (for he too was covered in soot) wrapped in a dishtowel.

"Come here," she muttered weakly.

Radha sidled up to her.

Aai settled the infant in her lap. Radha lifted a corner of her skirt and wiped the infant's face, gently.

Over the years there were nine children, one roving father, and Aai, a stone cutter with skeletal irregularities, who worked all day, often late into the evening. It was only natural that Radha overcome childhood, sidestep girlhood (with all its implied frivolities) and apply herself to the business of wiping noses, begging for food or scraping off stale bread out of garbage cans, and occasionally, when there was money, feed the little ones with glucose biscuits dunked in watered down milk.

Evenings were spent, either pulling out lice from hair matted with filth and patting the kids to sleep with stories of a heaven where you could pluck fresh bread right off the branches of trees, or massaging her mother's back with the heels of her feet, whatever was needed.

Now, years later, stepping out of the Solanki residence for onions, cilantro and three limes, per Cook's instructions, Radha, the maid – all her siblings having strayed like unwanted lambs the moment they were past the age of nine or ten – felt something, a lightness perhaps, an urge to lick the morning rays like *malai* with her lips, raise her arms in the air and swirl and swirl in a sort of one-person *ring around the rosie*, much like the little memsahibs that danced and played and lingered without care on canopied terraces, without aim or agenda.

Enjoying the moment, humming *tu mera raja, mai teri rani*, (you are my king, and I am your queen) as she took a left to the market, Radha, the maid toyed with the idea of treating herself to some tamarind drops tangy enough to make her teeth hurt.

Perhaps it was a rush of traffic just then, or perhaps it was simply bad luck, but a rush of wind directed the stench from a pile of offal, on the adjoining street, right into her face and made her stagger in slow motion, like the Bollywood heroines she so admired.

Squatting on the floor the way her mother had taught her, almost folding in half, Radha the maid, covered her nose with a scarf, broke out in a queasy sweat, steadied herself, clutching at the dirt, groaned, emitted a half-hearted belch, and finally purged her morning meal, right there on the sidewalk.

Kamla, taking in the pedestrians and bicycles cluttering and clattering on the sidewalk, remembered with a smile how she and Babuji, on a rare Sunday morning, walked along the same path to the corner taxi stop, to get to the city for lunch at The Ambassador before they caught the afternoon show at the Regal.

Kamla neither liked the lunch at the Ambassador, ridiculously small portions of finger sandwiches and milky tea followed by dissatisfying pastries, nor the foreign films full of needless sex that left little to the imagination, but she savoured the time spent with her husband and felt glamorous in the scarf and cat-eye glasses he so enjoyed gifting.

"You look like Garbo," he would tease and make her blush prettily. Kamla did not know this Garbo, but she knew a compliment when she received one.

Of course, this was before they had saved up for a car. These days she hardly ever walked anywhere again and enjoyed being driven around, but overlapping toes – a low grade although very real deformity – upset her balance and hurt her back, the exact day she touched forty, making it impossible to gad about, certainly never on high heels, on the bumpy streets of Mumbai.

Ishhhh! So hot already, she thought, hanging out her hand-washed lingerie in a discreet corner of the terrace. Kamla, like her mother and her mother before her, had been taught to wash her own undergarments, just as she washed herself each morning. It infuriated Babuji, Sami, even Radha the maid, that the lady-head of the household, should lower herself on the floor to scrub clothes in that unseemly fashion when they had a menagerie of servants paid to do the washing.

But we all have our compulsions, and some minor irritations must be endured to make room for peace. In time, they let her alone, whether it was with her laundry, her need to pre-soak and rewash the rice thrice in cold water before cooking despite the cook's irate assurances that he'd cleaned it already, or her excruciating presence at the doctor's office when he examined Atal.

"I need to see if he checks you fully. Last time he did not check your ears," she would shout above his protests. The poor boy cringing at the thought of his mother pointing and asking questions about his privates, begged Babuji each time to accompany him instead, only to be met with a sympathetic shake of the head.

"It's your mother's department, I'm afraid," Babuji always said. "She insists." And that was that.

"Atal! UH TUL!" A voice, part bark, part child, jarred Kamla out of her reverie.

She held a stern finger to her lips, then tilted her chin toward the front door.

Where was Atal anyway? She barely heard him these days and quite missed his childlike prattle, swinging his legs under the table long after everyone else was done eating.

Kamla, about to make her way down from the terrace, felt a touch of breeze and something soft and silky drop on her head and stroke her face as it fell to the floor. She picked it up.

Oye? A lace undergarment, a bra to be precise, so delicate and so explicitly red, Kamla had never seen anything like it, except in the western movies she watched with her husband.

It must be Khushi's, she thought. But she was such a modest girl! And if it was Khushi's, why was it hanging amongst Sami's things?

Kamla walked along the clothesline, fingering, checking each garment. Ah! Radha must have mixed up the laundry. She found Sami's and Khushi's and even some of her own clothes fluttering peaceably together on the line. Until of course, this itsy-bitsy thing undid itself from the clothespin and flew into her face.

Still perturbed, although she couldn't think why, holding on to the stair rail for balance, Kamla decided to shove the garment in the back of her mind for the moment.

She made her way to the corner bedroom and found it locked. Locked!

Atal was not old enough to close his door, leave alone lock it from the inside. Was he?

She knocked louder than she intended. "Are you in there, my baccha? Your friend is downstairs, waiting."

A muffled okay, a pause, then her son appeared, pale and semi-dressed.

"Are you alright?" Kamla touched his forehead. Atal jerked away as if bitten.

"I'm fine. Stop treating me like a child."

"Pshew! Clean up and go down at once! And don't use that tone." Kamla glared. Then she stomped off, but only after he had the sense to look shamefaced.

What is it with these children? A perpendicular crease popped on her forehead like a wayward line on an etch-a-sketch.

She was used to Khushi going up to her room and quietly shutting the door behind her. Although the child never failed to ask permission.

And Sami. Well, both the household and the walls of the house felt the reverberations when she slammed her door for privacy and locked it for good measure. Kamla wondered if she ought to take it personally. After all, she was the only one who ever really needed the children. When it came to Babuji, they went to him on their own accord.

And now with this undergarment business. Perhaps Radha would know. The girl had an uncanny ability to sniff out secrets and smears. Then she remembered Radha had come in from the store looking rather peaky and smelling of vomit. And Kamla had asked her to take the day off.

The concatenation of events led to something. But to what? She scratched her head. But as Babuji would say, she had nothing she could put into a report.

Still, like the smell, or the memory of a smell on your clothes after a visit to the crematorium, the uneasiness lingered. A little breathless, Kamla opened a window in her room. The wind that dropped the red undergarment onto her face, was now quite gone. But the tenor of her day, now as wobbly as her overlapping toes on the cool, firm ground, left her feeling unbalanced.

Sixteen

Babuji stepped on the cool, firm ground of his bungalow with the air of a man who was both master of his domain and slave to its charms.

"Ah, Kamla! How glad I am to be home," he said, thrusting the mandatory sari wrapped in brown paper into her arms.

Kamla wiped her hands on her tunic and accepted the gift, trying not to look too eager. She seldom went shopping for herself which quite doubled the pleasure of receiving.

"Did you not enjoy your reunion with your lawyer friends? We are having fish curry, okay? It's been such pleasant weather these past two days." She chatted, not caring a whit about the meandering nature of her conversation.

"Ah! Imagine floating on the backwaters in a thatched houseboat for two nights with eleven old men, who can neither handle a drink nor tell a joke to save their lives. I feel as though I've been unjustly penalized. Fish curry is fine," Babuji added with a sigh.

"This Sari is beautiful, Sri. Bright colour." Kamla was stroking the folds of her now unwrapped gift, the brown paper dropping heedlessly to the floor. "You are old too, na?" She added, but with a look that belied her words.

Babuji bent down to stroke his wife's cheek, doubled over and fell with a grunt at her feet.

It was Dengue fever. Perhaps a resident mosquito, restless in the moist interior of the South, had attached itself to Babuji's flesh, and come along for the ride.

Except for a mild headache, which he blamed on missing his breakfast coffee, Babuji had not experienced any symptoms, during the short flight home. Fortunately, Kamla, with her innate common sense and the wisdom that comes from being married a long time, summoned the Solankis' physician, apprised him with some dramatic flair of the fainting episode and had her husband quarantined even before his blood sample tested positive for the virus.

Like thousands of women before her, Kamla married young. Over the years, rooted in domesticity like a *Peepal* tree in the ground below, she knew of no other existence than the one she had with Sri.

Her heart was not her own, it beat for Sri. Her body was not her own, it functioned for Sri. Her blood warmed (and on occasion, boiled) because of Sri.

It was up to her to keep her heart, and her husband, alive.

After his fainting spell, Babuji was relegated to the bedroom where raging with fever and pressing his thumbs into his aching head, he thrashed about as if fighting a storm. Kamla sat by his side with cold compresses and acetaminophen and stroked his back and wiped his mouth after he spewed into a bowl.

No one, except Kamla and the doctor, was allowed near Sri.

She created a special diet of spinach soup, summer fruits, and a rice and yoghurt concoction and watched with a sinking heart when he shook his head. He did not have the strength to sit up. She put the food aside and kept him hydrated with coconut water, massaged his aching body with ayurvedic oil, muttering imprecations at the municipal authorities for not being vigilant enough, not controlling the mosquito infestation fast enough, and urging Babuji to get better as if it was a decision, he was loth to make.

Babuji, through a medicated, sleep-deprived haze observed the comings and goings of his wife and wondered whether he was getting better or worse. In one corner of the room, the outline of a young woman emerged, each time the curtains were drawn apart. She did not talk or move. Her hair was covered with a scarf, pulled tightly across her forehead like a hijab. Babuji wondered whether it was a ghost, a figment of his imagination, or Yama, the god of death, disguised as a woman, and awaiting his demise to carry him home. He was not afraid, merely struck by the mournful expression on her face.

Days later, His sheets were no longer soaked, his headache dropped from a level eight to a level two and the pain behind his eyes became a painful memory. The ghost disappeared.

Scarcely had the family uttered a collective sigh of relief, however, when a series of catastrophes shook the Solanki household to the core making even Babuji's Dengue a non-event, eliciting little more than a shrug response.

Years later, going through the desolate rubble of memories Kamla felt certain it was the anonymous note addressed to Khushi, leading up to the immediate dismissal of Radha, the maid, that was the nucleus of the storm.

Mumbai

Demons of the night.

Seventeen

Khushi pulled her top over her head, carefully extricating the stray hair caught on a hook, so it wouldn't break off. Then she positioned the table fan so that the breeze hit her face and bare neck.

Breathing a little easier, still sagging under the weight of four and a half hours of mind-numbing information, she wondered wistfully if there was a chance, she could save face by contracting whatever it was in the air these days, (except Dengue) and fall horribly ill before finals.

But Khushi was too well-raised to lie. Some might even say, she lacked the imagination. All she could do was sigh and hide in her room. And both those things she did, increasingly often.

Would Bali care if she failed her exams? She asked herself. She thought he might.

But not having discussed matters pertaining to her future with her fiancé, (Bali's sole focus these days was to divest her of her clothing) she did not have the answer to that question.

From the watchman's shanty wafted the heart-breaking voice of 'The nightingale' Lata transporting Khushi to vistas that were both melancholic and hopeful.

Her eyes welled, her lips trembled as sensuously as the lips of the screen actress belting out Lata's song, *lag ja gale*, (embrace me), to her reluctant lover, in the epic film.

Bali. What is it that you want of me?

The song took wing, caused ripples in the troposphere and transmuted into soothing rain. Khushi decidedly cooled off, pulled at the drawstring waist and wiggled out of her pants.

Perhaps Babuji wasn't home, she thought, or the watchman would get fired, for sure. "Turn off the radio. This is my home, not a bordello," Babuji would jab a finger at him.

And Kamla who usually felt the same way Babuji did, except at a more fevered pitch, would substitute the word bordello with *kotha* and assail the watchman with an operetta of ishhhh-flavoured reproaches.

Khushi, now smiling to herself, looked for comfortable clothes. Something that won't bite like teeth into my skin, she grimaced. All at once, her breath caught. Was it her fault the imagery was so evocative?

"Bite!" She whispered, touching her ear, her shoulder, her neck. Then blushing furiously, a little weak at the knees, she climbed into bed and tucked her naked body under the covers where she could safely regale herself with self-love. Once sated, she pushed aside the sweaty sheets and padded across the bedroom for a shower.

Ignoring the familiar headache, (a small side-effect of her harmless addiction) and dressed in a loose, cotton kaftan, she attempted to twist her hair into a clever little knot requiring just two long hairpins, when there was a knock on the door.

"It's a phone call from that studio where you applied for work," said Kamla, putting so much disapproval into 'studio' and 'work' one would have to be a block of wood to not notice.

"Thank you, Auntie," Khushi exclaimed, almost knocking a vase over in her hurry to get to the phone.

"Ishhhh!" Said Kamla, emphatically.

121

Kamla did not have to eavesdrop. Khushi, clearly not her usual self, raised her voice another octave.

"Yes. Yes. I will be there. Definitely!" She waited a polite moment before she hung up.

With a start, Kamla realized she had never heard that lilt in Khushi's voice before. Not even when it was Bali on the line.

Head lowered, the girl went back up the stairs almost knocking into Kamla this time.

"Oofma! Why so clumsy today?" Kamla scolded.

"Sorry. I was just thinking. Kamla auntie, would you do me a favour? Can you take me to Sami's tailor for some pantsuits? I think I will need some western clothes for this job."

"Of course!" Kamla flushed with happiness. "Of course, as always, I will help you, Child!" She squeezed Khushi's arm, a tad too hard. Khushi ignoring the co-conspiratorial tone accepted the squeeze graciously.

Khushi went up to her room and shut the door gently. She sat on her bed and breathed deeply. In and out. Her eyes welled up again. But this time the tears were not melancholic. I guess I'm not so useless after all.

It was just an unpaid internship in set design, but it was her chance to learn something, two days a week, and contribute to the dining room conversation, perhaps make Babuji, Maya, Bali, even Sami, angle their faces toward her when she talked, and recognize she was more than her body.

And someday, when she aged, she thought with a shudder, when the sexual undercurrents she created with her Madonna-like face and her fiery lip colour no longer fired Bali's imagination - she might need to become this other woman, a skilled and influential woman brimming with Maya's energy, Sami's insouciant wit, and her uncle's perceptive observations – that she may rein in her worldly lover, make him climax for her, only for her.

Perhaps, Khushi's brow creased, she ought to request more than a two-day workweek.

When Khushi had something on her mind, she knocked down and rearranged the accoutrements on her dresser. Now, she eyed the bottles of nail polish lying fallen like drunken sentries with distaste, and set about placing them all in a row. Her bindis, meant to decorate her forehead, dotted the landscape of the dresser instead, a colourful constellation gathering dust. Cupping one hand just below the edge of the table, she swept the sticky particles into her palm and placed them in the dresser drawer instead.

Tweezers, nail cutters, nail files and eyelash curlers, she decided with pursed lips, ought to lay on their backs like surgical instruments, on a paper towel, not quite touching. The lipsticks, strewn about like fallen wickets, must be housed, for the sake of sanity, in their very own box. Her hairpin box, she sighed with consternation, was not anywhere to be found.

Ah! There it was. Someone had placed a note on the side table and used her box as a paperweight. Why had she not seen it before?

Khushi put the hairpin box where it belonged and read the note once. She read it again before understanding dawned. Then, with a small sigh, softer than the susurrus of paper between her fingers, she fell to the floor.

Radha heard the footsteps, softer than the susurrus of paper, and felt her heart drop.

Before she could steel herself, she was upon her, Kamla, breathing smoke out of her nose, eyes like the pinpoints of a sword boring into her very soul.

"I haven't …" Radha the maid cowered.

"And you won't!" Kamla bellowed, raising an index finger in the air,

"Get dressed, and get out of my compound, unless you want Babuji to throw you in jail, you filthy, filthy girl!"

"But ..."

"NO! No words."

Radha, the maid gulped and dragged herself out of the watchman's shanty, snivelling. A cramping pain, in the pit of her stomach, made her moan like a bitch in labour.

"Why are you going toward the house?" Kamla struck her fist in the air.

"My things ... purse ..."

"Wait here. I will have them brought out. Do not step foot inside my kitchen, filthy thing!"

Something in Radha clenched. Perhaps it was the repetitive use of the word 'filthy' or perhaps it was something else, because the girl who mastered fellatio at the age of eight and danced bare-breasted before pimps-who-would-be-producers, for the sake of bread and watered-down milk, suddenly decided she had pride.

"You will not call me names, and you will tell me why you are asking me to leave," she said, her voice so steely, Kamla stopped short.

"Aiyo!" Kamla squeaked when she finally recovered. "Can you read? Do you see this? This is a note someone left in Khushi's room. It says you are pregnant. It says you seduced Bali. It says you are also the watchman's slut. It says ... Ishhhh!" The situation, the full ignominy of it suddenly dawned on Kamla, so that she had to fight for breath. Weakly she waved the damning scrap of information in Radha's face, then let it drop to her feet.

There was no sound now except for laboured breathing on the

part of Kamla, and shallow breathing – a bird at the end of its life – on the part of Radha. Between the two women, the note lay like a bad smell, a piece of turd shamelessly unflushed.

"I'm not ... I mean not anymore," Radha whispered.

Kamla glanced quickly at the girl pressing a hand to her stomach, her abbreviated pregnancy, and shuddered in disgust.

"I will leave," Radha said, more softly still, her eyes now dry and empty and ravaged as the Sahara.

And, with that, she did.

Kamla sat at her window watching Radha the maid make her way, past the house and across the street toward the bus stop.

It was a blazing hot afternoon and the girl, as far as she could make out, had no slippers on. Perhaps her slippers were in the house still, or perhaps she didn't own any, Kamla thought, distractedly. Despite her deep and righteous rage for the havoc the girl had unleashed, she felt a twinge of guilt. What kind of a woman, a judge's wife, no less, does not see to her maid's footwear!

The maid's head, Kamla noted, was uncovered. Every couple of minutes, she tugged at the loose end of her sari and used it to wipe her sodden face. With one hand she held on to a *potli*. All her worldly possessions, in a holdall the size of Atal's lunch box.

Kamla guessed at the contents of the holdall – a tin cup for her tea, a water bottle, a comb, some festive looking hairclips, sample-sized toiletries that Khushi and Sami let her have, perhaps some peanuts or black grams wrapped in newspaper, for her mid-afternoon snack, and a cell phone with a pre-paid SIM card that Babuji had given her for emergencies.

Glued to her upper-crust window, Kamla continued to stare after the forlorn creature. Unexpectedly, the memory of another Radha, a giddy-with-happiness, dancing-with-joy, Radha, rose in her mind. It was the day she showed Babuji the document that ensured she would get a flat in a low-income housing development, in exchange for her piece of land in the village.

"A *pukka* home. With on/off switches. With utensils," Radha had trilled almost bursting Kamla's eardrums.

At least, I gave her some money for pots and pans and such, that day, Kamla thought, feeling a little less guilty about the shoeless feet.

Finally, the girl's sloping, sunburnt back became a blur, until, hemmed in by an army of barefoot maids, she was cloaked in working-class dust and rendered invisible.

Babuji wished he could brush off stress like the dust on his jacket, with a simple voice command to his servants. Still, he reflected, mulling over his day in court, unlike the repeat offender, at least he had the freedom to return each day to his preferred retreat, over-sprinkled though it was with Kamla's verbal gyrations.

All in all, he reminded himself, he was a lucky man.

Babuji unbuttoned his coat. "Radha?" He called, puzzled. It was understood that the maid took his coat, offered him a beverage, and announced his arrival to Kamla, the moment he set foot in the door. The fact that Radha had quite ignored this unwritten rule and not made an appearance was an indication of something ominous, a serious breakdown in domestic machinery, perhaps.

Babuji wished he could simply back out the door and go somewhere, the movies, the club. But he remained rooted to the spot.

She will be here any minute and rant and ramble long into the night, he predicted, glumly. Now here she was – the love of his life, Kamla.

Kamla saw Babuji standing at the door and wished she had the courage to simply step into his solid arms and stay there forever. She was so tired!

"Ah! Sri!" She muttered.

Babuji waited.

Kamla, for the first time in her life, outwaited him.

"Is everything all right?" He finally ventured.

Kamla blinked hard. She never cried in public.

"I ..."

"Amma!" Sami called out.

Kamla blinked again, this time with surprise. "Sami, are you home?"

Sami opened her mouth. No. I'm a hologram.

Instead, she asked, "Amma, why does Khushi have a bandage on her forehead? She won't say anything."

"She ... She's hurt," said Kamla, then to Sami's horror, Amma made a fist, as if readying herself for an opponent and smote her own chest, succumbing to an eerie caterwauling that made Babuji's heart thud in his chest and the hair on Sami's arms stand on end.

A cacophony of bleats split the air.

"Ammaaa!"

"Kamlaaa!"

"Khushiii!"

"Radhaaaa! Get water!"

Maybe it was their bleating, or maybe she was simply out of steam, but Kamla screeched to a halt. Her hands dropped to her sides.

"Radha's gone. I fired her." She let out a pressure-cooker breath.

"Amma, did Radha hurt Khushi?"

Kamla's head went up and down in distracted assent. "Go sit with your cousin, daughter."

Then Kamla did what she wanted most to do. The unheard-of thing. She buried her head in the pillow of her husband's chest for all the domestic help, and her daughter, to see.

A dazed Sami watched as Babuji led his wife, clumsily, tenderly towards their inner sanctum.

It was all Sami could do, not to retire to her inner sanctum and bury her head in a pillow until she stopped shaking, stopped remembering her mother's horrific rendition of misery. Instead, she knocked at Khushi's door and let herself quietly in.

Her cousin was seated on her bed, teasing the knots out of her hair and staring out the window.

"Khushi," Sami said, "Would you please tell me what happened? You are hurt and Amma is beside herself and Radha ..."

At the mention of Radha's name, Khushi, seemingly riveted by the rush-hour traffic, turned a preternatural gaze at Sami.

"You have blossomed into such a pretty girl. And so thoughtful." She brought one finger to Sami's chin, rested it there for a moment, then withdrew it.

"Where is the old Sami?" She smiled, "The one who liked to taunt and tease and make me out to be the family dunce, ever since we came into your life nearly two years ago?"

Sami reddened, then quite forgetting she was supposed to be comforting her cousin, and not turning the conversation to herself, asked, "Was I so very arrogant? I am sorry."

"It's fine," Khushi shrugged her shoulders: "We invaded your home. Mother and I. Upset the balance, perhaps your footing in your family. You had a right to act out."

It was a conciliatory gesture, if not a whole-hearted acceptance of the apology.

Sami nodded slowly. Quite an observation from, let's face it... the girl who worries more about her pores than the rest of her life!

It was as though the two cousins lifted their heads out of the pool of self-absorption at the exact same moment, and were seeing each other for the very first time.

"So, did you fall?" Sami touched her own forehead, referring to the bandage.

"I may have. I don't know." Khushi sighed. Then she brought her face close to Sami, so close Sami could feel her hot breath on her face, and whispered, "Sami, did you write that note?"

"Note? What note?"

Sami's eyes widened.

"Has someone been writing to you, Khushi? Is that why Amma is upset?" Then with a glint in her eyes, "Wait! Is it a looooove note?" She puckered her mouth, as if for a kiss.

Khushi held her cousin's eyes, then, as if struck by an epiphany, her mouth still open, she turned her face to the wall.

Sami held her breath.

"He doesn't love me, you know ... Bali." The words dislodged, at last, pulsated in the space between them. The air grew heavy. Khushi's lids fluttered, then closed, exhausted.

Eighteen

Radha, no longer the maid, closed her eyes, exhausted.

Was the tear in the tarp roof bigger or was it her imagination? She was too tired to investigate.

In one corner of the hut, her husband sat on his haunches pushing around the bruised vegetables and bones simmering in a cauldron, with his left hand. His right hand was otherwise occupied - scratching his one inflamed testicle, until, irate, she threw her tin cup at his nether regions, to make him stop.

"What happened next?" He asked as if he was fully cognizant of all that occurred before. In reality, she had not yet uttered a word. But over the years he had learned to decipher the content of her silences. And this silence made him hot and cold in turn. This silence was about doors slammed shut, livelihood snatched, the maw of deprivation threatening to swallow them whole. What happened next was not really a question. It was a one-testicle man begging for the protection of hope.

Radha, when she was still a maid, found herself obsessing about Bali the moment he stepped in the door with a wedding proposal for Khushi. There was something suggestive about the way he fondled his moustache, bored his eyes into every female body in sight. It titillated, irked, and made her lose sleep. We are two of a kind, she thought every time she set eyes on him.

Radha's mind seldom latched on to a thought or an idea, buzzing compulsively instead from flower to honeyed flower. But Bali was on her mind as she tied and knotted her skirt in place before she left for work, dangerously below her belly button. Bali was on her mind as she thrust her husband's hand out of her *choli* blouse in the middle of the night. And he was on her mind as she swallowed the watchman's frenzied ejaculation, her eyes fixed on the Solankis' front door where Bali was so often found twirling his moustache and, insolently, without an appointment, ringing the doorbell.

It is not certain, the exact moment that Radha, when still a maid, decided she was going to stalk Bali. His movements were suspicious. His words belied his actions - he told Khushi he would be away on business, but Radha spotted him in the neighbourhood more than once. He was furtive and slippery, not like a thief but an adulterer.

He was insolent – she remembered how he made her scuttle to the sidewalk as he flashed past on his bike. Perhaps she decided she would follow Bali in order to seek sex, revenge, or both. Whatever the motive, it was a seminal moment that altered the course of many lives.

Bali, years later, wondered if he could've altered the trajectory of his life had he ignored the servant girl, standing motionless (except for those stalking eyes) under the Palace Motel – All R Welkom awning, and simply driven off with the tart-of-the-day leaning heavily on his shoulder.

But Radha, who seemed to appear everywhere those days, and found him always in a compromising situation, was beginning to make Bali uncomfortable. He enjoyed his new status at the Solankis' and was not about to jeopardize his position for a brazen, barefoot stalker who likely wanted baksheesh for keeping her mouth shut. So, he muttered,

"Wait there," tilting his chin at a pillar, and hurried as best as he could with his doped companion, to the side street where he was parked. He shoved the woman into the car. She flopped, sinking her chin into her chest, skirt riding up to her thighs. Cursing under his breath, he leaned in and tugged her into a more dignified position. Then he slammed the car door shut and walked with long strides to the waiting Radha.

"How are you?" Radha smirked.

"You are interested in my health? What the fuck do you want?"

"You, Sahib." Radha leaned forward. Her breath was sweet and cool. Mint leaves. "Only you."

Bali stared at the woman. She held his eyes, raised herself to her full height, widening her legs just a little and pressing her back against the pillar, poised for whatever came next.

Bali glanced quickly to the right and left.

"Solanki house, Wednesday," he said, mouth pulled into a rictus. "Send your watchman pal out on an errand."

Radha, on jellied knees, smiled weakly. Yes.

He showed up a few times, and took her without preamble, silently and with superb, aggressive ardour. Afterwards, she gave him the watchman's undershirt to wipe himself.

Then, he simply stopped.

"I was too busy."

"It's too risky."

And finally, "I am, let me see if I can put it to you in simple words, bored with you."

Not exactly gifted with intellect, nor schooled in sensitivity, Radha, nevertheless, understood humiliation. Especially when it was flung at her like excrement.

She kept to herself for a while. Lost herself in wishful revenge.

If only there was some way she could make him pay. Make him eat shit for the way he'd treated her.

Of course, it never occurred to Radha, when she was maid, that there might be a price to pay for her wrongdoings – against Khushi, against her own husband, and against the family that kept her employed.

Radha had no use for right and wrong. In her world, consensual sex was a private arrangement without legal, moral or religious implications. What was religion anyway? Just another industry designed to keep pundits fat and happy. Everything she knew about trade and religion, Radha learned from hiding behind the Peepal tree of the village temple in the dead of night, watching saffron-robed men trade food for little girls.

But she had not reckoned on this humiliation that burned like a flesh wound. It was her first time, you see – not the sex. We know that! But, Bali's rejection of sex – with her!

Silently, she licked her wounds. And bided her time.

After he'd had his fill of her, Bali saw Radha, when still a maid, hovering in the hallway as he entertained Khushi in her living room. Deliberately, he leaned forward, tucked a stray hair behind her ear, kissed her hand and laughed when she blushed.

"Oy, Radha!" He would call, now and then, just to see her face change colour, hope dance in her kohl darkened eyes. Then he would ask for a glass of water or a cup of tea, his lips curled cruelly.

After that, she left him alone with his fiancé.

Eight weeks after their last breathless encounter in the watchman's shanty, Radha, when still a maid, realized she was pregnant. Weeks later, she miscarried spontaneously. But Bali did not know that. Nobody did.

Two days after her miscarriage, still, a little shaken but confident, she decided to try something.

Bali, leaving his apartment building saw a flash of movement at his right.

"You!"

"Bali Sahib," Radha, when still a maid, pleaded, "May I have a moment of your time?"

Bloody nuisance! But mollified somewhat by her grovelling use of Sahib, Bali nodded, got into his car and started the engine.

"Hurry up, I don't have time."

"I'm ..."

The parking lot was not empty. There was the gateman, the chauffeur, random kids, a couple of women chatting, armed against the sun with umbrellas. Radha turned sideways, and shielding herself from prying eyes passed her hand meaningfully over her stomach, at the moment, flat as a washboard.

"Whose is it?"

She could not read his expression behind his Ray-Bans, but there was no mistaking the sneer in his voice.

She did not answer. Simply looked meaningfully at him. The fact was, she wasn't certain. And it was a moot point anyway – she was there to make him shit his pants. To make him pay.

"Well! What now?" He adjusted the mirrors before he looked at her.

Slowly she rubbed her forefinger with her thumb. Cash.

Bali, his face inscrutable, dove into his pocket and pulled out a wallet.

"Here."

The wad of notes exchanged hands.

Radha felt the thickness and heft of her bounty. He didn't seem perturbed, she noticed. Not even close.

"Thank you."

She tucked the notes in her bra, taking an awkward half-step. "If there's anything I can do for you ..."

"Wait," Bali said.

He found a sheet pad in his glove compartment and wrote something on it.

Radha wished she could read English. Read, in any language.

"You can do something. If you can place this note on Khushi's bed stand, I would appreciate it. Don't say it's from me. It's a surprise."

Radha looked down at the folded note.

"There's an additional baksheesh for you if you do this discreetly."

Radha wanted to say she didn't need his bloody baksheesh.

But she did. Need. So, she held her tongue and merely nodded assent.

Bali waited for Radha to turn around before he exploded out of the parking lot muttering expletives. Barefoot whore. You thought you could entrap me. Pig! Like I would touch your filthy hole, unprotected. Buy yourself some deodorant at my expense, bitch. Can't wait to see your face when they throw you out like garbage!

Radha, not completely satisfied with the outcome, (after all she hadn't made Bali cringe, not even a little) was gratified she had at least divested the shitface of some of his cash.

She found an excuse to go up to Khushi's room. From the sound of knocking pipes, Khushi was in the shower. You are delusional if you think he will ever want you, Miss *I'msofairandlovely*, Radha thought malevolently. She placed the note on the bed stand.

It fluttered and shook as if afraid. She looked around, found a hairpin box and placed it on the note just as she heard the shower turn off with a clank. The shower curtain rustled. Radha slipped out of the room.

Maya heard the doorbell ring and slipped out of the smoke-filled den, the hostess's smile still playing on her lips. The bell rang again. Persistent. She had sent the maid out for more ice thirty minutes ago, perhaps that was her, she would strangle her if it was, how dare she ring twice!

It wasn't.

"Sri! Ummm. I wasn't expecting you. Why did you not call?"

"I did. A few times."

Maya coloured.

"I'm sorry. I haven't been in much. And my new maid never gives me my messages."

Babuji waved away the excuse, "May I come in Maya, or are you going to let me wait here like a tradesman?"

Maya stared at her brother. He had never used his judge's tone with her before, assuming this prissiness was his judge's tone.

She stepped aside.

Babuji put his umbrella in a bin by the door.

"Of course. Although, I do have a few people over, including the irrepressible Batliwala."

Babuji sighed in irritation and stepped back. "Perhaps you better come on over instead, Maya. Whenever you can. Sooner rather than later. We need to talk about Khushi. How long has it been since you saw your daughter, Maya?"

Maya was beginning to get seriously annoyed. For a younger brother, Sri was being a bit too short with her. In fact, he positively reeked of insolence, calling her Maya twice with that specific, derisive inflexion.

Only moments ago, pressed against the door of her private bathroom Maya, in a lime-coloured gown, her face agog with excitement, had been told "you look like my favourite cocktail – only more intoxicating." She had a house full of happy guests, Batliwala was so pleased with her, that he attempted to pin a medal on her bosom – although it was a metal bottle cap, and he was decidedly inebriated. In any event, he was definitely sending a message to his team, that he liked her and they bloody well like her as well. She wouldn't be surprised if she got a better wardrobe and more responsibility in the coming season – Maybe, just maybe land front and centre as a news anchor. The very thought made Maya shudder with fearful happiness.

Now here was Sri, trying to put a damper on her evening, going on about Khushi.

"You forget little brother, that my daughter sees me at work at least twice a week. I'm the one who wangled her an internship." She said spiritedly.

"Sees you?" Dark circles shadowed his eyes.

"Have you another daughter I don't know about, Maya?"

"What the h ... whatever do you mean?"

"Khushi hasn't attended college or work for the past three weeks. She doesn't eat, drink or sleep. I think, perhaps, she is depressed. This whole Bali situation ..."

Maya frowned, perplexed. Had it been that long? Was there a Bali situation? Khushi was on another floor in the building, so of course, Maya wouldn't exactly bump into her in passing. But she was sure, she'd seen her recently. Perhaps even talked.

"Why didn't she call me or – or something?"

Babuji waved his hand again, withholding comment.

"Maya!" There was laughter and a call from within that turned into a riotous, drunken chorus: Maya. Maya. Come to me. Maya.

What must her brother think of the off-colour jokes, the unbridled laughter emanating from within, a small part of her wondered with embarrassment, until the other, more assertive part decided this was her home and she would not be embarrassed.

"I will drop by on the weekend, Sri. Sunday, I think. Give my best to Kamla. And do lighten up, you are overinvested in this parenting business, don't you think?"

Babuji's eyes did not waver.

"You may be right, Maya. Perhaps I am." The judge picked up his umbrella.

Over his shoulder, voice set to a slow boil, he said, "Certainly, a crime you will never be accused of – parenting."

Maya pressed a clammy hand to her heart, stood at the door until she heard his footsteps fade, then taking a deep breath returned to her guests, adjusting her mien.

Using his umbrella like a walking stick, Babuji adjusting his mien, crossed the street to where his driver stood leaning against the car, smoking a *bidi*.

"If you are quite done, may we proceed?" Babuji said softly, testily.

The driver, who hadn't seen Babuji approach, flicked his bidi in an open sewer jumped to a respectful stance, and pushed a dirty mop of hair away from his forehead, in one dizzying motion.

"Home, Sahib?"

"Yes ... I mean, no. I have one more stop to make."

Babuji directed the driver to a housing complex in Kurla.

He felt defeated. Not since his bout with Dengue had he felt so utterly without strength. Dealing with his sister was like witnessing an accident from the far lane, heart racing, wondering whether there were any survivors and if so, would they ever be the same again.

A cow blocked their path, staring moodily at the oncoming traffic: Bring it on. She lowered her head to drink from a puddle in the dented asphalt. Babuji knew the driver would not honk, would sit stoically, respectfully, until mother-cow had her fill.

He sighed at the complex, contrarian, communal spirit of his countrymen. Finally, the animal looked up. Made her infinitesimal way across the road. So, like Maya, he thought with a wry smile – her own rules. Her insatiable, self-destructive appetite. The car jerked forward. And suddenly, his mood shifted.

By the time he got into the lift, Babuji's breathing was even, he was his usual pragmatic self.

He pressed the doorbell. A servant let him in and had him wait in the living room. Moments later, Bali, flushed from a hot shower, made his appearance.

"I was surprised by your call," Bali said, choosing to sit across the sofa from Babuji. "Please excuse the mess."

He is being disingenuous, thought Babuji with distaste. Did he think there would be no meeting after his loathsome behaviour? That damning letter?

The servant stood by awaiting instruction. "I will have nothing," Babuji looked the maid in the eye, willing her to leave. She did.

"Bab ..."

"Bali," Babuji interrupted for perhaps the first time since he was made Judge, "This business with the maid has disrupted our lives enough. We are a family of some reputation and have no desire to disturb the social order. Your appetite ... your propensity to leap in the gutter, has broken my niece's heart. What's more, you were in my home. You exploited one of my staff. Do you realize what you have done you, foolish man? How uncivilized your conduct has been?"

"It makes us question, not just you, but your parents and their hand in your development. You are raised on mainstream values like most of us are you not? Do let me know if I'm missing something."

"I ..." Bali's complexion took on the hue of ginger root left to mould.

"I have asked Khushi to make very sure she still wants to marry you. She confessed to Kamla, she would like us to give you another chance. I have told her to think it over most carefully. She has agreed. My question is, do you still want to be married? Or is this all a ruse, the marriage simply an egregious way to prove your maturity and readiness for domestic life, so that you may continue to benefit from your father's wealth?"

Bali, who only ever saw Babuji peripherally, as a bystander in Kamla's living room, present at parties and functions with his ready wit, and occasional, genial rebuttal, shrank before the onslaught of insults.

The old man was going not just for Bali - *I make more money than God! I am an IIM graduate for fuck's sake*, his moral fibre, or lack thereof - but also his doting, unsuspecting parents.

He gaped at Babuji in a stricken way, not sure which question to address and how, and needing suddenly to pee.

"Well?"

"I ..." Bali's throat constricted. "I do like Khushi. My ... my parents don't, didn't ...what I mean is ..." he broke off.

140

The dithering fool. It was obvious the man had no defence. Babuji rose smartly from the sofa.

"It's settled then. Save your apologies. You have one more chance to redeem yourself. Then we will see."

I guess I will just wait and see how it looks. Sami, took a deep breath, holding up the outfit in front of the mirror.

Carefully, she tucked the starched white men's shirt in her waistband and centred her fitted black skirt so that the back slit sheathed each hip in poised symmetry. She stared at her reflection wondering whether the men's tie constricting her throat was stylish or merely Chaplinesque.

"Hello, are you from the catering service?" Bali teased as she came down the stairs.

"So funny. Haha." She made a face, then prettily stuck a red pointed toe for his benefit.

"Ever seen these beauties on a waitress?"

"Nope. Nor such rosy lips," he smiled, staring at her mouth.

Sami pressed her lips together, gently. Maybe I should blot the lipstick.

"Ishhhh! Sami! You look like a man. Go put on something else!"

Sami turned towards the peremptory voice.

"My! Am I actually the centre of attention today? Where's Khushi?"

Kamla pointed to her room, "Go!"

Bali raised a quizzical brow.

Sami stormed out the front door instead.

"But where does she think she's going? It's her birthday! People will be here soon!"

Bali, assuming her question was rhetorical, stood before Kamla poised as a butler, hands clasped behind his back. "Is there anything I can get for you, while I'm out? I'm going to replenish the beer and Campa."

Kamla eyed him with barely concealed dislike. *His expressions do not match his tone. Why did I not see through this fellow before? And that moustache ... leering at me. Indecent!*

"We have enough beer to fill a bathtub," she said, stonily.

She had complied with Khushi's wishes and given him a second chance. But fiancé or not, she would not treat him as before. *With a maid! Ishhhh! He had wiped his excreta-ridden life on her carpet and forever tainted her home.*

"I will be back, by the time the party gets started, in about an hour," he said quietly, the epitome of politeness, and was gone.

"**W**here did Bali go?"

"Ah, Khushi, you look radiant as always. He has gone out to get beer, or so he says." Kamla was staring dubiously at the furniture. *Those cushions look like they have been sat upon.*

"Do you not believe him, Kamla auntie?"

Kamla opened then closed her mouth. *Khushi was still so fragile, no point in disturbing her. Besides, she had a party to arrange.*

"I'm sure he will be back in a few," she smacked the cushions smartly before bookending them. *Ishhhh! What is that slipper doing under the sofa?*

"Oy, Cheetah, you look like a monkey. Go in and wash up

before Amma ishhhh's you to death," Sami teased gently, as she hailed a cab.

"What do you care?" Cheetah muttered angrily.

"What!" Sami started to say, but a taxi screeched to a halt almost at her feet, just then, and she got in without a word. Cheetah wiped the end of his wet nose with a kerchief, cricket bat wedged between his legs.

The cabbie honked off making pedestrians and feral cats scuttle out of the way.

"Atal, in or out? Last chance." Warned the Captain.

"Out. I have to get ready for my sister's birthday party," he said sullenly and left, striking at stray rocks with his bat.

The door opened before Atal could reach the doorbell.

"Hello there, Atal. What's new?"

To Bali's surprise, Atal looked at him exactly the way Kamla had, just moments ago – as if she wished someone would crush him under a heel, or, in this case, with a bat.

"You look kind of thirsty and I know for a fact there's no cola at home. Shall I get you some? I'm going to the store." Bali's smile had a cold fixity.

Atal shrugged sullenly, stepping aside to let Bali out, "Suit yourself." In the safety of the foyer, he blurted, "Khushi likes Limca."

"Does she now? You seem to know a lot about my fiancé's likes and dislikes. Tell me what else does Khushi like?" Bali bent forward with exaggerated interest.

His teeth are as big as a wolf's.

"She likes you to call first before you come over, and ..."

Atal added malevolently, "My mother and Babuji feel the same way."

"What about your sister? How does she feel?" Bali's voice followed him, taunting.

Atal, face contorted with rage, dashed up the stairs and to his room.

Khushi, having helped Kamla in her cursory way, straightening chairs, and plumping pillows went up to her room and sat on her bed, angling herself towards the mirror.

He seems different. Says he loves me. But has he changed? Or is this all an act?

The mirror revealed nothing. Just her dark-ringed eyes empty of sleep.

One by one, she touched the spots he liked to feast on – her lips, her neck, her left breast. All she felt was residual discomfort. A leave me be.

Khushi wanted the old Bali back. Correction. She wanted the prideful feeling of being affianced to Bali, of adorning his family album, plying his family coffers with her heirloom charm. Only, it no longer seemed enough. Of late, she wanted more.

She'd been watching a Turkish soap opera (with subtitles of course). The actor who could easily have been her double had imperiously rejected proposals from wealthy diplomats and celebrity designers, giving her heart instead, to a policeman who went down on one knee and (Khushi remembered every word) said, "If you will have me, I will spend all the days of my life trying to fathom the secrets of your soul. I will accept your tears as my failures, your smiles, my reward."

Equipped with knowledge obtained from the world of fiction, she reassessed her relationship with her fiancé. Bali, she admitted freely to herself, was more interested in locating the mole on her left breast, than learning the secrets of her soul. Not that she did not enjoy this compulsive need to caress. Usually, the very thought of it made her slide her fingers between her legs – but not today. Today, the thought made her want to shrug her shoulders as if shrugging off a fly. Bali did not care whether she smiled or teared up. Bali did not care.

They drifted back in slowly. Bali with beer, Sami with a chastised look in her mother's direction, Khushi with concealer under her eyes. The party was already in full swing – the judge's friends, tipsy, harmless celebrants clustered under a cloud of pipe smoke, Maya, like a slim glass of sherbet, poised on Babuji's chair, and Kamla with a furrowed smile and a watchful eye on the servers.

Sami, catching sight of Atal, with a slice of cake the size of a cricket glove, walked over to his side.

"Hey, I was supposed to cut the cake before you devoured it." She nudged.

"Amma said you wouldn't want to. Since you are so grown up and late to your own party."

"No, I'm not! I just went to the salon to get my hair washed."

"Are you angry with me, Cheetah? Did I forget to come to your match or something?" Sami whispered.

"No. Nothing. Go away."

"Okay." She said.

Atal watched her leave, although the look in her eyes made his throat hurt.

"Sami, why have you not invited any of your school friends?" Kamla asked perplexed.

"I don't have any. But here's Bobby now, all nice and neat in his khakis. Hi there! Would you like a coke? Limca?"

"Okay," Bobby said, his eyes on Khushi, propped behind an awkward piece of furniture, staring into the distance. Bobby Mehta was immediately transported to an enchanted realm lush with fauna, rife with bird song, perfumed with Khushi. And no Sami. Definitely, no Sami.

"Okay," he said again and Sami with an "Ooof" signalled the server.

Bali caught her alone at last, in Babuji's study, buried ostensibly in The Indian Penal Code, her forehead repellently damp.

"Khushi! Here you are. I missed you my queen, my heart!"

"Oh Bali. What's with the flattery." Khushi sighed.

Was that tedium he heard in her voice?

Bali was beginning to get a little fed up with this family. It seemed they had a hard time forgiving a little hanky-panky with the barefoot maid that he vehemently denied having anything to do with, in the first place. In Bali's world, it was the maid who was always in the wrong. Young masters were never suspect. And yet, here they were, the Solankis, getting into a flap over nothing.

In a rare display of anger, he was always so careful, he snatched the book out of her hand.

"The Indian Penal Code. Ha! And I thought Sami was the brains in the family. Planning a degree in law, hmmm? Is that why you have no time for your fiancé?"

He leaned closer, squeezing her against a wall.

"No time to make me welcome in this sterile, fucking ashram? Tell me, Khushi, have you found someone else at that part-time job of yours ... did you spread your virgin legs for a part-time lover? Was it good for you?" He was working himself into a fury.

His hips were grinding against her now, one large hand on her bony neck, making her gurgle and squeak like a rubber duck.

"Have you ever considered, it is your behaviour that drives me into the arms of another woman?" Bali battered on, getting louder and louder until a terrified Khushi, afraid someone would hear, someone would see, held her hands up to her face in abject surrender, her nose now leaking like a faucet.

He let up on her at last, looking with secret glee at the incremental devastation, the jagged breath, the wide doll's face falling apart like a child's jigsaw puzzle. How easy it was with women. Decimate them. Shred them like meat and shape them from scratch and voila! A tastier dish, a born-again housewife and ... (Khushi was on her knees, her head bowed) full-time servant. Bali felt himself harden. He bent down, put a finger on her chin so that she was forced to lift her eyes to her lord and master and with his other hand, pulled down her skirt.

From behind the walls, wave upon wave of laughter. Bali stood up. "Pull yourself together and join the party," he said averting his eyes from the wretched heap crumpled at his feet like yesterday's take-out. "And wipe yourself." He threw a tablecloth at her.

Sami, squeezed between Babuji and auntie Maya, was glowing with happiness. Maya had given her Joy: the most expensive perfume in the world. Sami had carefully dabbed a little behind each ear and felt immediately opulent. She couldn't stop staring at her aunt. There was something different about her. She was so stately, so impeccably turned out, she thought, with a sigh. But also, she was not, what was the word, as tightly wound. As if, whatever she had set out to do, she had done so, with aplomb.

Maya presided over the table in a pool of quietude.

Every face turned towards her and was instantly warmed. Serene as a coiffured Buddha, she offered a smile here, a word there, relinquished the salt, or pickle, like a favour that the guests accepted almost bobbing with gratitude. Now and then she glanced at Bali, her prospective son-in-law. To Sami's amusement, she saw the insolence fizz out of him like a balloon, leaving him flattened. He could barely meet her eyes, blushing instead like a schoolboy. Even Babuji's eyes shone with brotherly pride, as she teased and charmed his cronies.

Babuji presented Sami with a leather-bound journal. Sami moved her fingers on the gold lettering "The Pen is the lever that moves the world" Thomas De Witt Talmage printed on the cover. She loved the expensive, weathered look of the journal, craggy as the lines on her father's face; loved the heft of it in her lap, and couldn't wait to sit at her desk and fill the pages with profound, ponderous, world-moving thoughts.

Atal, with a shy smile, slid across to his sister, a pink change purse with a crudely drawn Mickey Mouse in cricket whites. He sat next to Kamla, working on his egg rolls, forgetting, at least for the moment, that he was still angry with her.

A delighted Sami reached across Cheetah and wrapped one hand around his glass. Carefully, she topped off his coke with some of hers. The dimple on his left cheek danced shyly in step with the dimple on her right.

Bali, a little flushed, told Kamla, sitting directly across from him, his fiancé was feeling under the weather and perhaps that's why had not joined them for dinner. Seated beside him, Bobby Mehta groaned as if in pain, then covered the sound with a cough. Kamla half-rose from her chair. Bali shook his head, bending one finger discreetly toward his nether regions by way of explanation.

"Ah!" Kamla said and settled back. "I will take a tray up for her, later."

"I will go up to my daughter," Maya said, looking directly at Babuji.

"Good idea," Babuji smiled.

Kamla flashed her eyes – about time.

"So, young man, when do you think you will tie the knot? We cannot wait to sample the wedding sweets!" Chortled one of Babuji's cronies in his phlegmy way.

"The delay is not on my part." Bali bared his teeth.

There was a silence at the table, rendered all the more uncomfortable as:

Babuji pressed his lips.

Maya cocked a brow.

Kamla fixed the guests with a glare.

To ease the tension, Sami decided she would like to blow out the candles after all. Amma gingerly placed a candle on the cut and mostly demolished cake and invited them to sing. Giggling, Sami too, sang along. The evening ended on a high note.

Just as she was getting ready for bed, Amma came in to wish her good night. Then to Sami's surprise, with a great deal of ceremony, she wrapped a pashmina (with a lingering, not entirely unpleasant smell of naphthalene) around her daughter's shoulders. Sami stroked the shawl. It felt soft, tender as a hug.

"You cannot get such pieces these days." She sighed. "My mother's blessing. Use carefully," she admonished tenderly, kneading, then resting her hands on Sami's shoulders a few seconds longer than necessary. Sami, sniffing reflexively, accepted her mother's treasured gift with a nod. That Amma would trust her, with something so deeply personal was a wonderful compliment and she appreciated it.

"So many years have passed, I can no longer smell my mother in this shawl. But she did touch it." Kamla's head went up and down, her eyes brimming with tears. "She is always with me, Sami. Her presence lingers in the mirror when I smile and I see her in your eyes when you look at me in a certain way. And, who knows, someday, I might even see her reflected in your children's eyes, their lopsided smiles, or in the way they incline their heads as they listen to your stories. Isn't that a nice thought? It certainly gives me comfort."

Sami nodded. "I wish I'd known her," she said. And Kamla looked at her as if it was her birthday not Sami's, and it was she, not Sami, who'd just received the most precious gift of them all.

Sami passed a reverential hand over the intricately woven paisleys. The shawl cackled with static making both mother and daughter jump.

Embarrassed, Kamla drew back and left for the kitchen, which was ishhhh! a regular mess.

Sami stretched out in bed, stuffed as a bear.

For all intents and purposes, she thought, turning off the bedside lamp, the birthday party was a success.

Nineteen

Bali, for all intents and purposes, was an unqualified success in the eyes of his parents, who viewed him not through the lens of character, but the evidence of worldly accumulations.

Mrs Mehta, a singularly plain, uneducated woman would hold up the fingers of one hand, like a child, and count off, one by one, how her Bali had his very own penthouse apartment, his very own club membership, his very own Audi – in other words, a success story, times three.

Mr Harish Mehta, a *khakhra* manufacturer turned investment banker, known (privately) as the H-bomb, thanks to his signature farts, was not given to forecasting outside his field of expertise, but you could tell by the upward tilt in his voice when on the subject of his son, that he too was pleased with Bali's performance trend, and felt assured he had made a sound investment.

When their son announced the wedding would be held off for a bit, his father assumed it was at Bali's behest and merely waved his hand as if the matter was not worth discussing, and mentioned, only in passing, that Khushi was a beautiful girl, but, what choice did she have? Of course, she would wait for Bali. After all, this was an arranged match. Leverage was everything. The Mehtas would decide the wedding date. All the bride had to do was appear on the set like a goddess – inaccessible, sacrosanct, awash in *shlokas* and designer clothing.

From the way events were shaping up, Bali, however, was not quite as sanguine as Mehta Sr. His revenge on Radha seemed to have backfired. The Solankis, having read the anonymous letter had sacked the maid at once, but were not so naïve as to assume he was the innocent one in that squalid situation.

The marked difference in Kamla – she had always been his biggest champion and in fact responsible for introducing him to Khushi, after all – was beginning to worry him. The way she puckered her nose and oof'd and ishhhh'd at him these past weeks was getting intolerable and had it been any other woman, Bali would have reduced her to dirt with his stinging condescension. But Kamla, like an obsolete household appliance, was made of sterner stuff. And even Bali could not berate her in her own home.

And then there was Babuji. The audacity of that old bastard brandishing his ridiculous umbrella, practically calling him a guttersnipe in his own apartment, and casting his parents in a bad light, still made Bali want to smash his fuckin' face.

But, there too, his hands were tied.

As a matter of vengeful fact, he, Bali, had made himself a fixture in the Solanki home – polite, charming, and attentive to a fault with his hand-wringing fiancé. But, just as he thought he was making real headway with doll-face, he found her choosing the company of Kamla, the kitchen staff, even the books in Babuji's study, over him.

Well, he wasn't going to allow that. And he hadn't. It was he who got to decide when and where they met and how he positioned her – pun intended.

"Bali?"

A hallway mirror reflected his leer.

"Coming, Ma." Bali reconfigured his expression to one of fond indulgence and followed his mother's voice.

"You wait, fucker," he muttered under his breath, "wait and see how I screw you over." But, whether the threat was directed at Kamla, Babuji, or some other member of the Solanki family, was unclear.

It was unclear why Maya, the mother of the bride-to-be was not privy to Bali's shenanigans. Admittedly, Maya was an odd piece, not quite fitting in the intricate, domestic mosaic crafted lovingly by Kamla. When Khushi received the letter, dropped to the floor, and sank into a sadness from which she never quite recovered, Kamla tended to her as if she was her own – with tenderness and lots of hot-and-sour soup.

It did not occur to Kamla to call Maya and ask her to look in on her daughter. The very thought was ludicrous. It was Kamla's firm belief that Maya lacked empathy (even when it came to her own daughter) and would only make matters worse for Khushi. However, when days stretched into weeks and the pallor on Khushi's face could no longer be blamed on lack of sunlight or poor nutrition, Babuji and his umbrella did pay Maya a visit. One which Maya still remembered with flaming cheeks.

Now Maya climbed the stairs, balancing a tray of buttered toast and lentil soup with one hand, managing her dress with the other, to visit her daughter. Why in god's name will the child not break off the engagement if she is so unhappy? She wondered.

Maya had a feeling the answer may have something to do with Khushi's childhood and was tempted to leave it there, unexamined. There are no walls so thick, that a child will not absorb the love that seeps through them. The same may be said of hate.

Her own history with her ex-husband, his extramarital trysts leading up to her revenge affairs, their final corybantic reunion in the moonlit bedroom, right before he slinked off into the night, never to return again ... was it any wonder it affected their daughter in strange, anxiety-fraught ways?

Maya, suffocating first in her marriage, then as a single parent, either ignored Khushi or used her as a weapon in her ongoing battles with her husband. We were careless with our only offspring, she admitted to herself, in a rare moment of insight.

Perhaps, Maya intuited, Khushi wanted Bali to give her what her mother could not - A man who would stay. A man who would make her a warm, weatherproof nest. But wasn't it obvious, that Bali was all wrong for the job? My poor daughter, Maya thought, like a leaf in the wind, letting the winds blow her where they will. Sighing tiredly, it had been a long evening, Maya knocked on Khushi's door and entered.

Despite the fact that Kamla had favoured Khushi with the most spacious room in the house, the room was dark and claustrophobic. Her first instinct was to draw the curtains. Shadows crept like bats along the walls and in the low light – the ottoman, footstool, hope chest stood like faceless gnomes guarding the wraith on the king-size bed.

It was also deathly quiet. Maya placed the tray on a side table with exquisite care. She realized she was holding her breath. Slowly she exhaled. Then gripped with unease, a tightness in her chest her physician would surely say was cause for alarm, she whispered: "Khushi."

"......"

Her daughter was not a sound sleeper. The slight rustle of curtains, the ticking of a hallway clock, even the swish of her skirt as she tiptoed up the carpeted stairs invariably found her clutching her thin nightdress, standing in the doorway, rubbing rheum out of her startled eyes. Yet, here she was, bending over Khushi's head, the snick snick snick of her high heels still echoing in her ears and nothing. No movement at all.

Maya felt a stab of fear. With thumb and forefinger, she lifted the duvet covering half of Khushi's face. Leeched of all colour, except for two beads of perspiration on her opal forehead, she looked lifeless. A yawn, a sigh, a trickle of drool. How encouraging the biological tics of those you love, when confronted with the possibility of death.

She pulled the duvet off, to give the child some air. She was sleeping on her side, head pillowed with one hand, her other hand resting on her stomach.

"Khushi?"

Still no sound her daughter heard her.

Maya pressed a cool palm on her daughter's cheek. Placed two fingers just under her nostrils. Felt the soft release of breath.

Slowly Khushi opened her eyes. She lifted her hand from beneath her head and lay flat on her back.

"I feel wet." She whispered, dully.

Her hands hovered over the stain spreading to her thighs.

"Khushi. Darling, I think you may have your period."

Khushi merely closed her eyes and drifted off. "Khushi." Maya ruffled her hair, rubbed her daughter's wrist. "You have to wake up. You are staining the sheets."

She pushed one hand under Khushi's back for traction and lifted her daughter until they were face to face.

"Come on, lower your legs to the ground," she urged.

Somehow, she got her daughter into the bathroom, somehow, she had her undressed, turned the faucet on, and waited for the tub to fill. Khushi sat at the edge of the tub, listing like a doll on dope. Maya held her for support.

Now, it was Maya sitting at the edge of the tub, as Khushi slid in, curled into a semi-fetal position and let the warm water lull her like a womb.

A slide show of memories: Khushi, at first light, nursing at her engorged breasts; the edges of Maya's shawl balled in her baby fist, one pink foot bare and wiggling, the other still snug in its knitted pink sock; Khushi, nestled between her parents, warm as bread – a babelicious troika of shampoo, milk and talcum becalming the air between them.

Abrim with rare sweetness, Maya watched her daughter soaking quietly.

Much later, she held her arms out. Khushi alighted the tub. Maya rubbed her down, handed her fresh underwear and a tampon, pushed her tired arms into a robe, and took her back to the bedroom.

"Stay here," she said, patting an armchair.

Maya changed the sheets and helped Khushi to bed.

"How about some toast?"

Khushi stared at her wearily as one would at a guest who overstays.

"Mama,"

"Yes."

"Could you leave now?" The rings under her eyes looked especially dark.

"I ..." a shadow passed across Maya's face, "Of course."

She shut the door behind her with a passive-aggressive click. So be it.

Before she left her brother's home, feeling a little peckish – so intent was she in making her presence felt she had merely toyed with her dinner – Maya decided she could use a little toast and some well steeped loose-leaf tea herself. Fortunately, there was no one in the kitchen but a desultory looking maid, wiping the dishes with an air of hopelessness. By the time she'd brushed a crumb off the front of her dress and freshened her lipstick, Maya had convinced herself the problem with Khushi, would correct itself. Things generally did.

The problem, in the world according to Kamla, was that there were only two types of people. Those who fulfil their duties and those who fulfil their needs. One might substitute 'passion' for needs, but it was not a word that she could summon comfortably.

Dinner was done, the house restored to order, kitchen mopped, children tucked in bed and, Kamla thought with a triumphant smile, Sami seemed happy, despite their little altercation earlier that evening. If only she'd dress more like ...

Kamla, with a start, realized she hadn't looked in on Khushi. The poor child hadn't come down to dinner, making Bali that moustachioed joker look, like an extra chair that disturbs the symmetry of an elegant table. She took the stairs, leaning heavily on the bannister to pull herself up and turned left to Khushi's room to bid her good night.

"Amma."

"Atal, why aren't you asleep?"

"I was. I had a bad dream."

"Why didn't you go to your sister?"

Atal shrugged sulkily.

"Okay. Go back to bed. I will say good night to Khushi and then, I will have a story for you."

His eyes widened. Atal loved his mother's stories. Lately, she had treated him like a big boy and rarely sat with him by his pillow until he fell asleep.

"Go," she shooed him with a smile.

Sighing imperceptibly, Kamla entered Khushi's room, forgetting as always to knock.

Khushi was sitting up in bed with moonlight casting a halo on her head, the pallor on her face unnatural, even for her, making her look abject as a widow. Kamla shuddered involuntarily.

"Khushi."

Khushi turned toward her aunt.

Kamla felt her chest constrict. Not the most demonstrative of women, she found herself taking the girl in her arms, kissing her forehead, "God be with you ... God be with you."

"I'm okay. I will be fine." Khushi muttered into her aunt's lap.

"Ah! But I want more than that for you, dear girl. I want every *khushi* in the world for you."

Khushi looked up, her ringed eyes full of foreboding, "Kamla auntie, whatever happens, I want you to know, you are the only person in the world who treats me as if I matter."

Kamla, speechless, stared at her niece and quite unexpectedly, began bawling like a child.

For a few minutes, there was no sound in the room except for the unladylike blowing of noses.

"I will close the curtains, so you can sleep better," Kamla said after a while and Khushi gratefully sank back into bed.

What in God's name is that indecent man still doing outside? Kamla taking her time with the drapes glanced furtively below. Bali was standing across the street, conversing with a motley group of taxi and rickshaw drivers. She could see a cigarette gleaming between his fingers. Suddenly he moved forward to talk to a passing woman.

Surely that was Maya?

"Ishhhh!" Kamla uttered, then clamped a hand on her mouth. Khushi appeared not to have heard. Her eyes were closed. There was a blue cast to her face, an ethereal quality that made Kamla's heart jump to her throat.

She glanced outside again. Maya was getting into a cab. Bali held the door for her then stuck his head inside the taxi window, for more frivolous chatter, Kamla presumed.

They are two of a kind. Kamla looked around as if startled by her own observation.

Head bowed, feet protesting with each step, Kamla limped to her bedroom, then turned back around ... Atal!

Like Khushi, Atal too was sitting up in bed, except there was far more animation on his face. Clearly, he did not feel the need to clear his bed of comics, candy wrappers, colouring books and the like, simply pushing them aside with his feet. Out of consideration for his mother, he had cleared a little space for her as well, kicking off pieces of Lego and other hard toys so that they landed on the floor.

"Aieee! How untidy you are!" Kamla exclaimed but made no move to bend down and pick up his stuff. She simply did not have the energy.

"Which story will you tell me? Is it a new one?"

"Let me think, umm, yes, it's new."

With a deep, contented sigh, Atal settled back on his pillow. He hoped his mother would stroke his hair as she sometimes did.

'There was once, this little girl ...'

"You?"

'No. Another little girl. She and her brother lived in a small house no bigger than a kerchief, in Kolkata, by the river, Kati-Ganga.'

"Like you!"

'Yes. But quite far from where I lived. So, this little girl loved her family and she loved the life she was given. It was a simple life.'

'Every weekday she went to school with her brother. They walked past a temple, and her brother would bow his head to the goddess, and the little girl, who thought her brother very wise indeed, would bow her head as well.'

'They would pass by a sweet shop and her brother would buy a snack and offer her a piece. He would thrust his in the pocket of his shorts, and she watching him, would thrust hers in the pocket of her skirt.'

"'For later,' he would say."

"'For later,' she would nod."

'They passed a goat tied with a string to someone's doorway. Her brother would let the goat nibble at the grass with his hands. When he was done, the little girl would offer the goat some grass and let her nibble it with her hands.'

'At school, the children parted ways. He to his class and she to hers. He would wave at her, just before he turned a corner, a short, quick wave, almost as if he was brushing off a fly and she would wave back, a short, quick wave as if she too was brushing off a fly.'

"She loved him," Atal said.

Then Amma nodded. The nod went on for a bit.

"What happened next, Amma?"

Amma stroked Atal's head.

'In the evening, the little girl and her brother sat on the kitchen floor on a mat, and their mother sat by the stove, rolling out bread,

dishing out curry and rice and yoghurt to help the food go down.'

"Did their father work late, like Babuji?"

"Yes. Just like Babuji," Amma agreed. Her hand rested on his head as if she was taking a break.

Atal nodded intelligently.

'One day, the little girl noticed, her brother's plate did not look exactly like hers.'

"'Why is his plate so full and mine isn't?' She asked."

"'Because he is a boy and growing rapidly.' Her mother said."

'The little girl nodded; her brother was indeed growing rapidly.'

'A few days later, on a Friday, the little girl noted, her brother had two vegetables and some spiced fish on his plate. Her plate did not include fish.'

"'Why is there no fish on my plate?' She asked."

"'Oh, you won't have an appetite for it,' her mother said."

'The little girl did not know what it meant to have an appetite, but hoped, someday she would acquire it. The following week, and every week thereafter, for as long as she could remember, her brother was served fish every Friday, and she was not. Years later, the little girl's brother left home and joined the army. There was a war with China, you see ... and there he ... he died.'

"Were they all sad?"

"Yes. Very. Very." Amma nodded. This time she did not stop nodding for a long time.

"And then?" Atal prodded gently.

'Then one day, the little girl, now a young lady, and her father – who was home early every evening since he lost his son – got ready for dinner. The girl caught the delectable whiff of spiced fish even before she

sat down. Her mother apportioned two vegetables and a large helping of mackerel onto her daughter's plate.'

"Yay!"

Amma stroked his face.

'The girl stared at her plate in awe. Bedecked in colour borrowed from ripe tomatoes, hot jalapenos and earthy turmeric the mackerel arrived like a celebrity guest, turning her humble meal into a banquet fit for kings. And it was so wonderfully prepared, not runny in the least, thickened with coconut, ginger, garlic, all her favourite spices. She tested the fish with her finger. It flaked easily, tenderly. She tested a morsel. A complex host of flavours exploded in her mouth. It tasted every bit the way she knew it would, from watching her brother who always sat on her right, his legs crossed, his back straight, his forehead gleaming with adventure, working his way through the fish. And after he'd licked his plate clean, he invariably smacked his lips. A big, appreciative smack that never failed to make his mother smile. The girl picked up a morsel then changed her mind and pushed her plate aside, instead.'

"But why Amma?" Atal was sucking his index finger sleepily. Amma extracted the finger out of his mouth.

'The girl said: You are right, Mother, I do not have an appetite for fish.'

Amma looked down at Atal. But he was fast asleep. Wearily she tucked him in and left the room like one who had no appetite for fun, flavours and feasts.

Babuji had quite lost his appetite for fish. As a matter of fact, he thought, pushing his plate despondently away, life has no flavour anymore.

Kamla was upstairs, snoring mightily, having tended first to Khushi, then to Atal. This, after a long day of cooking and entertaining a group of people who had no more bearing on her life than a bunch of gnats buzzing over her daughter's birthday cake.

"You look like a hot water bottle ... but collapsed," Babuji chuckled, knowing full well, that Kamla did not react well to his particular brand of humour. But, she'd merely turned on her side, too drained to respond.

For a few minutes, he watched his wife as she slept, her mouth slack, stray swatches of orange and grey hair matted over her face. Kamla was experimenting with henna and other organic hair dyes. Unconsciously, she scratched the back of her head. The pillow was speckled with dandruff and dead skin. Her sari had ridden up, exposing a slab of unshaven leg. Her breasts flopped on her belly.

A feeling close to revulsion swept over Babuji, followed almost immediately by guilt. He loved Kamla. That she looked the way she did, at this moment, should not make him care for her less.

Meditatively, like one renewing his wedding vows, he checked off the attributes that made him love his wife so much, her devotion, her ability to give and receive love, her pragmatic ways. But then, the Kamla who lay beside him shifted her well-nourished body and emitted an impressive belch, evicting the gentler, nobler Kamla reposing in his mind. Babuji placed a calming hand on his wife's forehead. She quieted down. Small puffs of air escaped her mouth like tentative, warm-up notes from an amateur's instrument. Quickly the notes gathered momentum, grew to a crescendo and before he knew it, the walls reverberated with the sound of her snores. It was then that he turned off the light and headed for the kitchen.

He covered his plate with a dishcloth, preferring not to make eye contact with the dead-eyed fish he'd nibbled at just because he couldn't find anything suitable in the fridge. After a few, still moments, he left.

He was at his desk. Perhaps a little reading, he thought dispiritedly. Something unfamiliar, that he may lose himself in for a while.

Hmmm! What have we here? He tugged at the slim, motheaten book squeezed shyly between Malraux and Maugham.

Marvell! Babuji laughed hollowly. Yes, there was a time when he read poetry – when he was neither Judge nor Babuji, but simply Sri – a lad who dreamed with eyes wide open and saw a woman etched in the stars. He leafed through the pages until his eyes fell on

To His Coy Mistress. Ha! He cocked an ironic brow heavenward, then read:

... My vegetable love should grow
Vaster than empires and more slow;
An hundred years should go to praise
Thine eyes, and on thy forehead gaze;
Two hundred to adore each breast,
But thirty thousand to the rest;
An age at least to every part,
And the last age should show your heart ...

His staccato voice, like a parrot's echolalia even to his own ears, succeeded in distressing him almost as much as Kamla's trumpeting. Babuji turned off the lamp, and sank back into the absolute darkness, shielding his heart against the demons of the night. A few still-born thoughts later, he felt with the tip of his index and middle finger in the groove of his neck along the windpipe. Yes, there was a flutter of a pulse. Just barely.

Twenty

He was barely conscious, having treated himself to an evening of surreptitious drinking, when he saw Radha, no longer the maid, dart to his window like a winged lizard or a sequined ghost roaming the pitch-black skies.

"Ram ... Ram ... Ram ...," the watchman chanted the name of God, faster than his chattering teeth.

"Open the door, you idiot, it's me, Radha ... not a ghost."

"Wait. I have to urinate," said the watchman, plucking at his shorts.

Soon she was sitting cross-legged on his bed, there being scarcely any furniture in the shanty.

"Why Radha, you look great, like an expensive prostitute," he said, salivating freely after he'd lit a cautious lamp and looked at her more closely.

"And you look exactly the way you always did, Horsedung," she retorted, pleased at the compliment.

"Tea?" He poured a glass of hot, heavily sweetened tea out of a flask.

She accepted it

Soon they were talking, sipping and savouring the warm spaces between words.

"Are you making money?"

"More than before. Although, all this shit is expensive," she ran a hand down at the sequins glued onto her satin crop top, her nylon skirt, the frothy scarf around her neck.

"How about one for the sake of old times?"

"Okay."

"Really? No charge?"

"Unclothe yourself, you piece of dung, before I change my mind."

It feels like home, Radha thought, playing lazily with the watchman's pecker, listening to the sudden drumbeat of rain.

An hour later, the skies sucked back the downpour and the part-time nester shifted to her own side, restless.

"More tea?"

"Yes."

This time there were a couple of biscuits as well. They munched companionably.

"Listen. I can come around more often if there is something you will give me."

"What? I have no money."

"Keep your money, Horsedung, it's information I want."

They talked a little more, then sealed the deal with a satisfactory rubbing of groins, before Radha, not a ghost, slinked off into the forest of the night.

The night sky hung over him, an upside-down dome, fraught with consequences. Bali knew he had committed an evil act. He was not repentant. But he wished he could undo it. If the little pipsqueak dared utter a word to that shrill woman, Kamla, so soon after the Radha incident, there was no doubt in his mind, that Babuji would descend on him like a ton of judicial bricks, and make his life a living hell.

A bolt of lightning followed by an Armageddon roar of thunder scared him off his bed and nearly out of his wits. What the f***!

Trying to still his shaking hands, Bali lit a cigarette. Three inhales later, he felt a little more like himself.

I need to formulate a plan, just in case little Khushi opens her mouth, he thought. Stubbing out his cigarette, he tried a few scenarios:

Scenario one. Denial:

Khushi has not come down for breakfast or lunch. She has locked herself in her room. A harried Kamla threatens to break down the door and have her niece carted off to her clueless mother if she does not open the door, right this instant.

A reluctant Khushi opens the door. Kamla takes in her slipperless feet, her face the colour of breast milk, her slight frame shaking in her thin nightgown like a firefly caught in a glass bottle.

"Whatever is the matter with you, Child?" Kamla holds his fiancé by the shoulder, but not too hard, afraid she will break.

"It's Bali. He raped me," Khushi sighs and falls to her knees.

Kamla lifts her niece's face, detects the truth in her abject face, fights a wave of nausea and swears vengeance.

A menacing voice over the phone requests the pleasure of Bali's company at the Solanki residence. Bali arrives with a bunch of roses for his beautiful Khushi.

Kamla thrusts his bouquet into the hands of a maid as if it is ridden with lice.

The judge confronts him. Bali is appalled.

"Your niece lives in a fantasy world! Perhaps she watches too many daytime soaps," he sneers.

"Do you really think I would take advantage of her, in her own home, with a room full of people behind the walls?" He challenges.

"How stupid do you think I am, Sir? I was on the Forbes 30 under 30 list!" He roars.

That ought to shut them up. But maybe not. Khushi was not a liar. She had no agenda. One look at her haunted eyes, the Judge would believe her.

Bali lit another cigarette. If I come out of this incident unscathed, I will buy her one of those diaphanous nightgowns, a size too large, to accentuate her fragility, then make her swoon once again ... pass out in my arms from sheer happiness.

His heart rate quickened, and his hand went to his member.

Scenario two. Unapologetic acceptance:

A menacing voice over the phone requests the pleasure of Bali's company at the Solanki residence. Bali arrives with a bunch of roses for his beautiful Khushi. Kamla looks at him witheringly. The flowers wilt in his hands.

The judge confronts him. Bali lowers his eyes. Blushes before the great man and confesses.

"Yes. We had sex. We are consenting adults, Sir, are we not? Your niece has not been herself. She flits from a home she doesn't belong in, to a college she doesn't care about and a job that's leading nowhere with a listlessness that is frankly unappealing. I was trying to resuscitate life into her. To assure her, above all, that she has my support. I was being a good lover."

Nah. Doesn't ring true. He is a judge. I can't pull off that bullshit with him. And it's her vulnerability against my word. He will find a way to throw me in jail.

Scenario three. Repent:

A menacing voice over the phone requests the pleasure of Bali's company at the Solanki residence. Bali arrives with a bunch of roses for his beautiful Khushi. Kamla dumps them on a corner table with unnecessary force.

The judge confronts him. Bali lowers his eyes. His lips tremble.

"I ... you see ... I am so in love with my fiancé. And lately, I have been under a lot of stress. I needed her. I... She is the love of my life, Sir. It will not happen again, I assure you. Not until we are married, at least. Forgive me."

Bullshit! Dither before that old fart with Khushi probably listening behind the door, seeing me behave like a mouse? Not going to happen.

The room was beginning to fill with smoke. Bali opened the window a crack. The wind whistled in, filling every corner with a furious, anguished rime. He pulled the window shut again, sank back in an armchair and thought some more.

Scenario four. Turn the tables:

A menacing voice over the phone requests the pleasure of Bali's company at the Solanki residence. Bali arrives with a bunch of roses for his beautiful Khushi.

Can you put these in a vase half-filled with water? He asks a maid peremptorily. She takes the flowers out of his hand. Curtsies.

Kamla arrives. "I have a meeting with Babuji," He shuts her up before she has a chance to speak.

The judge confronts him.

Bali raises himself to his full height.

"I will not dignify your accusation with a response. I see what you are doing, Sir, you are trying to break off the engagement and save your niece's reputation in the bargain. Perhaps you cannot afford to give her the send-off she deserves?"

"I will shame her publicly. I will ruin her, unless you apologize to me, this minute. Me? Rape? It was she who led me by the hand to her room. She who made the first move. And, let me make myself clear, she was still a virgin when I left. If the circumstances have changed since then ... if she has been with another man, tell me now... so that we can drop this farce forever."

Bali slapped his thigh as if slapping a winning horse. The odds were not so great, the engagement might still break off, and Khushi, his gorgeous, wind-up doll could slip through his fingers. But screwing over a pompous judge and his ridiculous soulmate ... priceless!

Stubbing his cigarette in the ashtray, he went once more to the window. The sky, a deep shade of ominous, cast an exploratory moonbeam. Stray dashes of light cut through the city.

Bali took his shirt off and ran his hands over his chest, his torso.

You are quite a specimen, aren't you? Somebody said that to him recently. Very recently. At the time he'd treated the remark as a compliment laced with sarcasm. He was used to such digs. Now he wondered whether it was something else. The more he thought of it, the more he was convinced, there was a suggestiveness in the tone and in her eyes that he had ignored at the time.

Well. If that's the case ... A fearful pleasure shot through his body, making him convulse. He looked down at his rock-hard member. Filled his mouth with air. If that is the case, he thought nervously, then it is quite the win-win, isn't it?

⸺⟨∽◈∾⟩⸺

Sami tucked the envelope into her bag. Even if I don't get into an Ivy League school, I would still be getting as far away from home, as possible. And that is what I call a win-win, she thought. For the nth time, she wondered if her college application cover letter was too personal, too whiny, too grade school, even for a middle-of-the-road college in New York. But it was the only draft that felt honest, and, she decided, at last, would have to be enough.

It was late. She had been up, sending draft after draft into the computer bin, when she thought she heard a noise. Following the sound, she walked down the hallway.

This time she heard a low moan. It was Atal, thrashing about in his sleep.

Sami stood over her brother, a sentinel in pink pyjamas, much as she had done when he was still an infant sucking his fingers, his Yoda face all scrunched up, whether in pain or gladness, or gas, was anyone's guess.

Are you okay? She whispered.

She knew they'd knocked him off the street cricket team. That his request to participate in the school play had also been refused. And when he dragged his defeated body off the school bus – someone had written LOSER with a sharpie on his bookbag. Naturally, Atal believed the bully. It was, after all, the way he felt.

With a lump in her throat, Sami remembered how hard Atal tried to fit in and the way his little face lit up when she rechristened him Cheetah –the fastest land animal in the jungle.

It had done wonders for his self-esteem, she smiled, still a little proud of herself for having thought of it.

She bent down to stroke his hair. One day, soon, baby, these rickety legs will carry you far, farther than anyone has ever gone before, just you wait! She rose from his bed.

Amma was in Khushi's room. This, Sami gathered, because

Amma was always in Khushi's room. She imagined Khushi squished like a hot dog, in Amma's doughy arms. Sami's eyes welled with angry tears. Two girls sit at the table, but only one gets the crumbs of your attention. She stood uncertainly in the hallway, then walked back to her room for yet another rewrite of her college letter:

```
I am the older of two siblings. Spindly,
dark-skinned, hair like rope, fraying at the ends.
Not exactly supermodel material.

My little brother, too, has his own set of
problems.
```

She typed, almost without thinking.

```
Born a preemie, he has been wearing corrective
glasses since the age of three. His teeth fill his
mouth like abandoned, crooked wickets, and do him no
great service in the looks department.
```

The thoughts came fast and furious.

```
I am, for better or for worse, a role model for
my brother. And I want to make him proud.

What I hope to recover from the humanities
program, she typed, is a mind, unfettered by biases.
I believe that despite the colour of our skins, our
less than perfect teeth and our humiliating sports
stories there are still great and good things, that
we can accomplish. With the right education. That
we need not be stowed away by parents and society,
like participation certificates, gathering dust in a
corner of the attic.
```

Words flew out of her like homing pigeons released in the air. A few feverish minutes later Sami stared at the page in front of her.

In the final paragraph, (thank goodness, they want no more than one page) she said being away from home would be as much a relief for her as an education. That she hoped, through the diversity of cultures, commonality of languages, and arguments of philosophy she could arm herself with truths and fight the good fight for not just survival but a glorious life.

As I said at the start, I'm no one's idea of a
supermodel. But I do believe in the superpowers of
a sound education. She ended with a flourish and hit
Save.

Sami stared at the letter. When it struck her at last that it was really done, she screeched out of her chair and pirouetted out of her room into the hallway and back, I finished! I finished! I finished! I finished!

She returned to her desk, stared at the letter, added one comma deleted another, and admired the clever way she had knotted the last two sentences. Then hit Print again. The printer went into action. The letter appeared with a whirr and a whoosh.

Maybe I ought to share the cover letter with auntie Maya. Sami sighed, suddenly racked with doubt. She pulled the envelope out of her bag. It looked tight-lipped and official, as if it no longer belonged to her anymore and prying it open would be tantamount to tampering.

Well. Can't do anything. A fait accompli. She shrugged and returned the envelope carefully to its hidey-hole in the bag.

Maya side-stepped the day's mail cluttering her doorstep, and still somehow managed to pierce a sepia-coloured envelope with the steel tip of her stilettos. She pulled the frayed cover off her shoe with one hand, walked across her living room to the kitchen cabinet in three long strides and shot the offending article in the direction of the couch where it fell, like an origami bird. I could murder for a drink, she sighed. Expertly, she uncorked a bottle of wine and poured herself a glass. Then another. When the knot in her trapezius muscle didn't show any sign of relaxing, she poured herself one more glass – third time's a charm.

"Aaaah!" Maya kicked off her heels, shrugged out of her jacket and stretched out on her couch, wiping her lips with the ball of her thumb. There was something scraping her back. Cursing she drew herself up, unhooked her bra, and felt around. It was the envelope she had dropped en route to the wine cabinet.

Maya tore open the cover, smoothed the paper with both hands and stared at it befuddled. Surely it was a mistake. How very juvenile! She repressed a giggle, despite being alone and in the privacy of her home.

Someone had drawn the outline of a heart, on a blank card, then coloured it carefully with a red-hot crayon. A cupid's arrow (leafy green) burned a hole through the heart centre, in a very precise fashion, as if alignment was everything.

Maya turned the card over. Nope. No message. She looked again at the cover. Yes, it was addressed to her, but in an unrecognisable hand.

Well! Be still my heart, she grinned. That's exactly what I need. A pimply kid in ripped jeans and a talent for colouring between the lines, to f*** my brains out, she muttered crudely.

Maya held the drawing at arm's length, for another moment, then let it throb against her chest, closing her eyes. The wine cure appeared to have worked. Her muscles uncoiled, loosening their grip on her neck and back. A soft sigh like a bird surrendering to its fate escaped her lips. The fine lines under her eyes and between her brows decided to take a sabbatical, release her of cosmetic woes. Light as a houri, she floated out of her worldly body and wrapped herself, newly slick and satiny soft, around the firm hips of a nameless boy in faded blue jeans, for a few magical hours. Lub dub music filled the air.

When she arose, she felt the need for a cigarette. It was just as she was about to reach for her pack, that the doorbell rang.

Maya glanced at the clock. It was past 11 p.m. Not exactly

visiting hours. She answered the door. Her hand flew to her heart.

It was him.

Twenty-One

Khushi answered the door. Her hand flew to her heart. It was Bali. Despite the muddy monsoon sky, enough shards of sunlight poked through the clouds so that, to her fevered mind, he glistened in the doorway like the messenger of Death.

"I have something to ask you," she whispered.

"May I come in first?" She drew aside.

Bali walked into the living room. The call he's been expecting from the judge never did happen. Already, he had put the incident behind him. There was a buoyancy to his step Khushi found quite unsettling. In fact, the more she looked at him, the more certain she became, she knew nothing of this man.

"Ask the maid to get me a drink, will you? Chilled beer would be nice."

Khushi, already seated, did not get up, gestured for him to sit down, instead.

"Well?"

Bali's eyes narrowed. He leaned back, tenting his hands as if readying himself for a wasted exchange with a junior clerk. Bile rose in Khushi's throat as her eyes fell on the dark fur between his shirt cuffs and wrists. His shoes looked freshly polished. Bali was the sort of man who did not have his shoes polished at home but preferred to raise his foot peremptorily on a wooden box on the street and have a menial squatting on the floor, wax and shine each shoe and glance up, every now and again, with an abject mixture of fear and humility to gauge whether Sir was satisfied with his efforts. It was only after a final swipe with a cloth dampened with the man's spittle, that Sahib, having examined each shoe from toe to heel, put a hand in his pocket and threw a few coins on the floor.

"Are you going to tell me what's on your mind, or are we playing a guessing game?" He finally asked, when the silence between them grew thicker than smog. And to think he had started out so recharged, so full of bonhomie when he left, that morning!

So, she told him.

With one eye on the front door of the Solanki home and the other on his mobile phone, the watchman kept abreast of both domestic and world affairs.

So far, that morning, he did not see any action on the domestic front. Bali came by and was let in by his fiancé. All menial help went through the back entrance, the security of which, was under Cook's jurisdiction.

With a loud yawn, the watchman looked down at his screen, hoping to find something titillating to pass the hours.

He finally found a stripper with perfect musculature slithering up and down a rope, doing a chesty forward shimmy between each exertion.

He was about to settle back, a leer still playing on his lips, when the unexpected happened, making him jump to his feet. The front door of the house, firmly shut thus far, burst open. A red-faced Bali shot out, turning around once to scream expletives in the air. "Never! Never! You two-timing little tart, will I accept this. It's over. OVER!"

The watchman shot out of the door and landed on the doorstep almost before the second OVER. It was his job, after all, to know what went on in the household, so that he may protect the occupants, sure, but also, so that he may keep his promise to Radha, not a ghost, and pass on everything he had on the Young and the Slimy.

"Is everything alright, Sir? Can I ..."

Bali Mehta expressed his sentiments by landing a blow to the watchman's face, so vicious, it brought the poor sod to his knees.

"I ... you ..." the watchman held his head, in a desperate attempt to understand what just happened.

But Bali had already reached his car and disappeared with a slam. The front door of the house, however, was still partly open. The watchman attempted to crawl towards it, possibly to shut it, or perhaps find succour within its walls when, through a fog of pain, he saw Khushi, like a disassembled doll, also on her knees, also trying to crawl away from the scene of violence.

In the relative comfort of his own bed, the watchman nursed his wounds. Two days later, the burning in his jaw receded. Instead, his mouth (now minus one snaggle tooth) turned to ash and a small flame, more an ember really, glowed in his heart. Not given to Big Data, he ignored the danger. As was bound to happen, the flame grew, blazed, took on the dimensions of a forest fire, and raged through every crevice of his body. Fire consumed his soul.

For the first time ever, he thought of Radha, the ghost, with something bordering on empathy. So much more than a glorified sex object, he wiped his eyes, pensively, here was a well-rounded, real-life character, just like him, with hopes, dreams and a thirst for vengeance. Now that he understood her obsession with the Solanki family, she wants to find a way to hurt them, of course, she does! He vowed to commiserate and fully support her.

Together, he thought, shuddering from head to toe, together we will bring Bali, that sister fornicator, down.

The watchman stoked his rage, readying himself.

Three days later, there was still no sign of him. This infuriated him like an itch he could not scratch. To avoid the salacious distractions of YouTube, he tucked his mobile phone under his mattress and kept both eyes peeled for the Arsehole.

It was the tail end of the third day. The watchman twisted and turned on his hard stool with growing discomfort. A close examination of his derriere revealed he had an acute case of haemorrhoids. Not having any poultices or alcohol to numb his pain and very little money for medication, his temper, (combined with his itch for revenge) hit a new high.

Unfortunately, Kamla, unaware of his discomfort, unaware even that the watchman had suffered any injury thanks to her precious (alas! Soon-to-be) son-in-law, chose that moment to come by with one of her petty demands.

It was only a few yards to his shanty but Kamla was out of breath.

"Oye, Watchman," she pointed insultingly, "Why did you not bring eggs for tomorrow's breakfast? Go now before the shop closes!"

"It's Gopi!" He snarled.

"What? Who?"

"My name is Gopi. Not, Oye Watchman! You can call me by name from now on." Then he locked eyes with her, and nearly bared his teeth, and interestingly enough, it was Kamla who blinked first.

She laughed nervously. "It's been so long... I'd forgotten your name." She turned her back on him, a trifle shaken.

"Nobody likes to be forgotten, Amma," he threw at her, insolently, "not even a watchman."

"Fuuuf!" Snorted Amma and waddled indoors, wiping her face with her scarf only when she was behind closed doors.

The watchman watched her go. The confrontation with his mistress felt like a cold compress on his fevered brain. There was, however, a small tremor in his right hand, when he pulled out a smoke. About to strike a match, he heard his mobile phone, still tucked under the mattress, let out a strangulated sound.

He retrieved the phone just before the caller rang off. It was Radha, not a ghost. Magically, the tremor stopped.

The watchman (you may call him Gopi) provided her with an update. Together they reviewed progress, devised strategies and agreed on the economic forecast. All in all, it was a productive call.

Judge Solanki was in his study when Kamla marched in without knocking.

"This watchman, he was rude. Very rude!"

"Why?" Babuji looked up, his reading glasses giving him a historical flair.

Kamla paused, nonplussed, then shouted, "Does it matter? He is the watchman! I am the ..."

Babuji closed his eyes.

"Do tell me exactly what happened, Kamla."

"He ... I asked him, very nicely, Watchman, we need eggs for breakfast. And he glared at me! Then he said, his name was Gopi and I should make sure to call him Gopi, not Oye Watchman."

Babuji nodded, getting the gist. He stared at Kamla, a small smile hovering on his lips. It made her insane.

"Don't look at me in that Gandhian way, Sri! I do address the menials by their name if I can remember ... but his tone! And why now? I've always called him Watchman!"

The judge looked thoughtful.

"Who is to say when the spark of self-respect glimmers in

someone else's soul?"

Kamla's eyes pierced into her husband's soul. And found it wanting.

"Yes. Do call him Gopi. It is his name, after all." Then the judge went on, placatingly, "And let me know if he insults you with a look, or word, again. I will take care of it."

"Ishhhh! Always, you will take care of it, why not right this minute I will take care of it ..." she muttered, not completely satisfied the judge was on her side.

The judge went back to his work with the satisfied air of a Head of the Household, muttering something about domestic storms in proverbial teacups.

Kamla, however, did not get a chance to dwell on the watchman, Gopi's angst, for long. And Babuji put it out of his mind, altogether. On the following day, there was a power outage, caused no doubt, by severe lightning conditions the night before. The entire neighbourhood was shrouded in darkness. There were no stars that night, nor fireflies flitting like exclamations of hope or fleeting joy.

Also, Khushi killed herself that same night. And, the world, as the Solankis' knew it, came to an end.

Mumbai

Between her living and her ending,

my one misstep.

Twenty-Two

It is my fault. All of it. She was in my charge. I left her on a black night, alone with her black thoughts.

Why was she so sad? Why could I not make my Khushi smile?

It was I who introduced her to that devil, that Bali. I brought him into my home and into her life and I fed her to him on a plate, piece by piece.

The power outage. It was as if, it turned the lights off in my stupid brain. Looking for candles and flashlights. Preparing a meal in the dark because Cook disappeared, who knows where.

Sami and Atal sat huddled with Sri in the study. It is where they had their meal. I ate alone in the kitchen. I left a plate for Khushi on the dining table with fish fry and rice pudding. I cut up some fruit for her. I always do, you see – Apples. Bananas. Mangoes.

The darkness. It deceives you into thinking you are tired. I went to bed. I did not check on her as I always do. My touch, my smell, my voice in her ears just before she went into the night, would it not have given her some sweet comfort, like mother's milk?

She did not come down for breakfast. I did not go up to check on her.

Between her living and her ending, my one misstep.

It was I who found her at last. The servant was shrieking.

"Kamla, memsahib, Khushi's door is locked. She is not answering," she said.

This is what I saw:

I went up. Gloom lingered in the doorway like a smell.

I did not knock or call out. I cannot explain the feeling of dread. I simply suggested we break open the door. And there she was.

A puppet on the string of fate. A scarf thrown over the ceiling fan to create a noose. A footstool kicked to the side. Her face drooping like a flower, the stem broken.

The room, then filled with people. And so much noise.

My Khushi is silenced. My fair angel. Daughter of my heart. I feel her absence like a barren womb.

How will I face her mother?

Twenty-Three

Let's face it. It was Kamla who found her. I, her own mother, was not around. Never around. Why should that come as a surprise? To abdicate responsibility, that is, after all, my speciality.

It was Sri who notified me. By the time I arrived, she was laid out on a stretcher. The horror of seeing your child, evicted from life, carted out like debris, incinerated – because you showed no care.

I cannot deal with this. How shall I deal with this?

I did go up to talk to her, that one time. What an evening that was. Sami in a tux, licking cream off her fingers. Sri, amicable, affectionate even. I was the life of the party. La belle dame sans merci. Across the table, I watched Bali watch me like fresh dessert.

Khushi did not come down to dinner. I took her up a plate. She had wet the bed. Or perhaps, she had her period. Dear God, how did I not see, there was a problem? My self-absorption is boundless. My ambition was all-encompassing. It left no room for Khushi.

I helped her undress and get into the tub. I washed her back. I know I loved her like a mother, then. Or, maybe loved the memory of myself as a mother. I suppose I travelled back in time to cup her infancy, gather her scented innocence in my hands.

Then, my daughter turned me away. "Mama, could you leave now?" Too little, too late, is what she meant.

Khushi, darling Khushi, do you forgive me? I would have loved you more if I only knew how.

Who were you? What moved you? I looked at you and saw only a blank canvas. Your beautiful face that I thought was flesh and bone, and little else. And yet, a face can hide as much as it can reveal. Was it not my duty to probe your depths, drain from your body, your self-disdain? Why did I not think to hold a mirror to your face, show you who you really were – a miracle, a child of God, a thing of joy.

You were all I had left. And I let you go.

That night after I left the party, I was looking for a cab. Bali appeared out of nowhere – a cigarette between his fingers, an enigmatic smile on his face. He opened the door for me. When I settled inside the cab, he stuck his head in. Good night, sweet Maya, he slurred. I ought to be insulted, I replied. But he saw that I was not. His breath was warm on my face. His lips were full.

"You are quite a specimen, aren't you?" I said, drily.

He did not quite know what to say. I lifted a hand to his cheek and pushed his head roughly away. Inadvertently, deliberately, my finger grazed his lower lip. I asked the cabbie to get a move on.

A light shone in Khushi's window. Someone is watching, I remember thinking. Was it you, my Khushi? Did you see something? Sense something? Is that why you are gone?

It was never my intention to hurt my child. My husband left. I was desperate to get out from under my brother's wing. Khushi was safely housed. That's all I cared about. I should have known that a child, unlike a pet, needs more than a warm spot, an occasional cuddle. Kamla was good to her. But I was the mother. And I was absent. I let her down.

Only last week, I was at the gravesite of a friend. Writ upon her grave were the words:

The giver of joy from 1935–2016.

And here I am. The giver of despair. God help me.

Why was she so lost? Did she really love Bali? He is neither a lovable nor a loving man, this much I know. God forgive me, I slept with him.

Twenty-Four

We were sharing her bed, sitting cross-legged, playing Snakes and Ladders – the floor was wet and Khushi didn't want us to leave prints on it. "Let's not increase the maid's work if we can help it, Atal," she said.

Khushi was kind and considerate. The best-prettiest.

I let her win, once or twice, in Ludo. She was always so pleased as if she'd scored a sixer. She did a little dance then tickled me silly. We laughed all the time.

The first time she came to our house, my knees felt weak.

She was so beautiful. So fair. Sunlight fell on her hair like a golden waterfall. Her eyes took in everything. The house, the garden, the family. Her hands were clammy when she bent down to say hello to me.

I would have hugged her, but Sami held my hand tight.

"Here comes Atal ... Here comes Atal ..." she would shout with delight when I entered her room.

"Sami calls me Cheetah," I admitted to her once.

She was quiet for a moment. "I like your name... Atal. You do know it means firm? Resolute?"

I nodded.

One day, I went to her, to show her my second–place trophy for Track. I was so dirty, so happy.

She looked like she'd been crying. Her eyes were red.

I went up to her and patted her head, the way Amma does when I'm upset.

She put me on her lap.

"I wish I could grow little. Become like you. Be anyone, but me," she said. There were still some tears trapped in her lashes.

That made me sad. I told her, I thought she was perfect.

"You are my best friend, Atal," she said, quietly.

I think I was her only friend.

Amma loved her very much. I asked her once if she loved Khushi more than she loved Sami. She became quiet. She pointed to her gut, "Sami lives here." Then she pointed to her heart, "and Khushi, here."

"And what about me?"

Amma smiled and kissed me all over my face ... "Do you really not know, little mouse?"

Amma is perfect too. All she ever wants from us is to eat more, rest more, do homework more. And to keep smiling.

Khushi stopped smiling soon after she was engaged.

We didn't play much after that. Her room was always shut. Sometimes I could hear her crying if I put my ear to the door.

That morning after the blackout, Amma broke down Khushi's door. Then we heard her scream.

Khushi was hanging from a fan. She had tied her neck to a pink scarf. Amma had given her that scarf at the time of her engagement. Her long hair was down, unbraided like Rapunzel's. Her face was lopsided. She had a clown smile like something out of a scary movie. Her eyes reached into her head. She looked terrifying.

It's a joke, I thought. It's a Khushi doll. It's not Khushi. Then there was more screaming.

Everyone stood staring up at Khushi, afraid out of their minds. Then Babuji shouted for help in a strangled voice.

Somebody was on the footstool, trying to pull Khushi down. Then Sami was in the room. And I knew.

I just knew why Khushi did what she did.

Twenty-Five

She did what she did. I cannot come to grips with it. The finality of my niece's death. I can hear her distress shriek through the night, I feel her desolation, like a widow's veil, cloud the day.

I am the householder. The Judge. The family's health rests on my shoulders. I cannot afford to behave like this... this demented old man who howls at the moon and hears elegies in birdsongs.

Kamla has taken to skulking in shadows, overcome with black thoughts. I urge her to get some sun. She says she does not deserve the light. Atal wets his bed. And Maya is a shell of her former self. All her ambition, her bravado gone. She has taken time off from work, does not even pretend to fix her hair and sits on a rocker all day, smoking, cursing. I fear for her sanity. My sister is in mourning. Once she was my rock. Now she is a survivor. Ridden with guilt.

I have decided I will remove myself from public life. I watched my family from the comfort of my study, walled myself with books, too superior to enter their messy lives. I am a criminal. I committed the subtler, more insidious crime – the crime of absenteeism. I am no better than Maya. Simply, more self-righteous.

How can I be of any use in court? I, who flounder in my erudite fog, a bewildered, impotent man.

The first few minutes were chaotic. Horrific. Kamla screaming, beating herself, passing out. Cook and the cleaning woman scurrying around, not helping. Atal standing in a pool of his own urine.

I asked them all to leave. Called a senior police officer, I knew from the court. They arrived almost simultaneously – the forensic pathologist, the police and the ambulance.

I'm not sure who let Maya know. Was it me? Thankfully, she was spared the sight of her daughter suspended in the air like someone's idea of a macabre joke. By the time she arrived, they had already lain Khushi on a stretcher, her hands folded on her stomach, in a semblance of dignity.

After a few simple questions, like *"Was she depressed?"* and *"Did she have any reason to take her life?"*, I answered, "Yes. And yes. Some trouble with her fiancé."

Then they assured me with lowered heads, that an autopsy would not be necessary. I suppose, my status of a Judge had something to do with it.

One of the detectives, on his way out, asked me in no uncertain terms, if I'd like to have the fiancé 'dealt with.' I knew what I was saying when I looked into his eyes, "Do the necessary." And so did the detective. I realized I could be charged with ill-intent.

Unlike my Kamla, Maya stood rigid, staring at the wall, obviously in shock. In the harsh morning light, her zig zag life projected cruelly on her face. I could not help her. Help any of them. There were deep ligature marks at the back of Khushi's throat. Somehow, this shook me more, this desecration, more than anything else, more even than the sight of her, looking down at us, her mouth set in a terrible rictus, her legs hanging uselessly in the air.

My world has caved in and I am struggling for air.

Khushi. Child! Forgive me. I thought your troubles were ordinary. The sighs and tears of a romantic heart. I did not view them seriously enough.

And take my forgiveness as well. Yes, you need forgiveness. You showed a callous disregard for your life – a sacred privilege granted by God. Thou shalt not kill. You have ignored the fifth commandment. How could you do that?

The sun does shine again and the air does cleanse. It fills me with rage, that you could not get past your woes and would not ask for help. How could you sink into this poet's despair when you had seen so little of the world? Optimism is the ambrosia of youth. It may grow rancid with war, with illness, with extreme old age. You had not earned the right to give up on this world! You had no right, Khushi!

I left it all to Kamla, pleased that she did not treat you as just another guest.

My kindly, worn-out wife. It was not enough she was in so much pain, but she had to be the one to answer a phone call, the following day, whilst we were still struggling with arrangements, the rites and rituals before the funeral. It was from your doctor, Khushi. Unaware, you were no longer among us, she complained that Khushi had not kept her appointment. She said you were seven weeks pregnant.

How and when did this happen? Why did you allow it? Did you allow it?

Kamla, my poor Kamla. You were her cherished star. A pristine example of virtue and loveliness, for Sami to emulate – the ground has fallen out from beneath her feet! How she rues the day she introduced you to that evil man. I must seek her forgiveness.

Kamla, you did warn me, the children might stray. As always, I mistook your concern for prudishness.

Let them have their youth, I said. They are bitten by love. Let them delight in this fleeting season. How could I have been so foolish? Where did my broad mindedness get me? Where did it get Khushi?

I must lift myself. Walk across the void for Kamla's sake.

My daughter. Sami. I do not know what to make of her. If Khushi has broken my heart, Sami has rendered it unfixable. What was it that Atal said? Was he hallucinating? He screamed, he wet his pants and when he saw Sami, he cried: It was you. Your fault. I saw you with him! Was my son crazed? Did the sight of Khushi hanging from the ceiling fan, affect his tender mind?

No. There was truth in my son's eyes. And in my daughter's eyes, a shameful secret.

I make no excuse for what happened next, although I am told it was a form of seizure ...

My silver girl. I cannot look you in the eye.

Twenty-Six

He would not look me in the eye. My father. And he was right They were all right. Babuji, Amma, Atal, auntie Maya.

They say the universe is very vast. That infinity is space without measure.

My universe was the size of Babuji's hand. His hand is mapped with journeys, I will never learn about. Together we skirted the potholes of tradition so that I may arrive at the doors of learning. Babuji.

Amma's hand, in mine, was large and warm. Like a cuddly toy, but unbreakable. She stroked my hand. With dutifulness. And joyless patience.

My Cheetah's hands were small and eager. The colour of play. They pulled me towards the playgrounds of imagination. Together, we fluttered and floated in countless fields, with boundless joy.

I do not recall auntie Maya's hands. But I do remember her fragrance. It wafted in before her, a bouquet of enticements, and long after she left, I could sniff her scent on my fingers. I know she treated me as an equal – a partner in crime. And, in the end, it was she who saved me.

Khushi's hands were like milk and snow. Before I touched them, they were gone.

Martin. My husband. Do you really want to hear my story? It is a short one:

Once upon a time, I had a family. We held each other tight. Then they let go of my hand. The end.

Do I miss them? Indeed, I am under their spell. They walk beside me – during the day, ghosting with the wind, and lie between you and me at night, shape-changing in my dreams. And yet, they elude me.

If only I could stay awake long enough, or fall asleep long enough, or master that state between death and consciousness long enough, that I may be with them again.

Atal. Little Cheetah. I do not know how much you saw when you saw us. How confusing it must've been for you. How painful! Know this. I would sooner cut off my limbs than see you hurt in any way. You were mine from the moment you were born, mine before you were weaned off Amma's breast. I miss the dimple on your left cheek. I miss your dorky games. I miss running with you in the rain. You, who loved me most of all. Until you loved Khushi.

I was up half the night watching Boys Don't Cry. Afterwards, understanding enough to be deeply disturbed, I tossed and turned for a long time. It was a very warm night and almost dawn before I fell into a sodden, restless sleep. My dreams have always been intense. I remember violence, gunshots, and finally, falling from a very great height until I roused myself, as one often does, in the nick of time.

Naturally, I was even more discombobulated when I thought I heard Amma screaming. It took me a good minute or two to process that I was awake. That it was almost daylight. That the noise and screaming was not Part 2 of a dreadful dream sequence.

I pulled a shirt over my head and staggered out of my room. The hallway lights were on. A group of people huddled silently outside Khushi's door in various stages of panic. Then, without warning, the screaming started again. This time, it was a collective keening that almost hollowed me out. I took one step back, wanting desperately to hide somewhere until whatever it was, was over, when another cry, like a baby rabbit trapped in a T-bar snare, stopped me in my tracks. Atal! I found my feet.

She was hanging like a piñata, from the ceiling fan. Her noose was bridal pink, her death grin like a slap in the face. A nightmare come to life. I felt the ground slipping. Someone put a protective arm around me and held me up. Across from me stood my little brother, the whites of his eyes giving him an otherworldly air. I felt his rage prickle my neck.

"It was you. Your fault. I saw you with him!" He shrieked. His spittle flew in my direction.

So, you know. I closed my eyes.

Despite the harrowing circumstances, Babuji absorbed our one-sided exchange, formed a hypothesis and solved the case, without missing a beat.

"What did you do? What did you do?" He shook a fist at me, his body juddering, so unstable the watchman held his arms out wide, hoping to break his fall.

We stood without breathing, without moving a muscle, Amma, I, even Atal, eunuchs before his wrath, hoping the turbulence would pass over our heads. I am not certain what happened next. Perhaps, Babuji forgot he held a stick, or perhaps the need to find justice for Khushi, and penalize someone, even if it meant his own daughter, was so great, he lost control. All I know is, his walking stick shot out of his hand, headed across the room to where I stood weaving, and slammed against my left hip. I fell to the floor. And stayed there.

Babuji wouldn't look me in the eye.

When I came to, Khushi was being carried out on a stretcher.

There were policemen and medical staff everywhere.

They spilt out of the house to the front yard and moved into corners, frowning gravely.

Later, men in white tunics and pants appeared, formed a line, folded their hands as if in prayer, awaiting direction.

Women I had never met before, arrived in droves, all clad in white. Some beat their chests. Others threatened to faint. But mostly, all eyes were lowered. And all heads bowed. Auntie Maya disappeared somewhere.

Chairs were brought out, tea was served, and phones were set to silent mode. All of Babuji's cronies sat bundled at one table, nodding to themselves, their old-fashioned banter trapped in sombre coughs.

Amma sat rocking on the patio floor, a collapsed mess. Right before my eyes, she turned into a decrepit old woman. Another woman, with very little hair, thrust a book of scripture into Amma's lap. The book kept sliding off, flopping to the side. The balding woman kept pushing the book back on Amma's lap as if there was a point. As if, everything would fall into place, Khushi would rise from her bed, stretch out and greet the day with her bland smile and velvety eyes, and we would all pick up our lives exactly where we left off if only Amma would spread open the Ramayana, in her ample lap, in the acceptable fashion.

After that, it was all over.

Babuji pleaded ill health and retired from his duties. He could be found in his study at all times of the day, staring at the same page of the Iliad, or was it the Odyssey?

Amma went away for three weeks to an ashram, also, ostensibly, for health reasons. When she returned, she looked about the same – like one of those heroines in a black-and-white movie, dying of consumption.

Upon her return, seeing that we were fed and clothed and appeared healthy enough, she went away again, whenever the mood struck her, which was often.

Auntie Maya locked herself in Khushi's room for days, weeks. She looked like death warmed over, herself. Then she returned to her apartment. We did not see her for months at a time.

Cheetah spent most of his waking hours atop a tree, with a pair of binoculars and bottled water. I believe he was researching the migratory habits of Bluethroats and Sandpipers.

I continued to apply to colleges outside the country. We were, each of us, a little island, lost in a windless routine.

It occurred to me that Khushi had never taken up so much room in our lives until she was gone.

Then, one day, auntie Maya reappeared. I know she wanted to talk about Khushi but regaled me with stories about work, her social life, and her travel plans instead. Her face looked parched. Joyless.

"Why are you really here, Auntie?" I finally asked, surprising myself with my bluntness.

"Did Bali ever visit?" She asked, colouring a little.

"No."

She dug inside her tote bag, passed me a piece of paper, a news clipping: Bali Mehta, son of Medha and Harish Mehta, was found in the parking area of a seedy little establishment in Juhu, called Palace Motel. According to one police source, the young man was beaten, tortured and left in a coma. He is in critical condition.

I hid my shock as best as I could, shrugging noncommittally.

"What happened between you two?" She asked.

"What makes you think something happened?"

Auntie Maya looked at me wordlessly. I saw no trace of judgement on her face. Only sadness.

I blinked back tears. She put a hand on my cheek. And I unravelled, "Some truths are easy to digest, Auntie, others, not so much."

Despite Babuji's belief that I could be anyone, do anything I set my eyes on, I learned very early on that I would never win a Nobel prize. I would never be a Playboy bunny. I would never dream in colour. I would never be enough for Amma.

Amma took care of all of us. She was, is, diligent in her duties. My hair was never left unbraided, my lunch box always replete with seasonal fruits, fresh veggies, dairy, and a B-complex vitamin instead of candy, for dessert. She still keeps tabs on our routine check-ups. Atal has dental and vision problems, and of course, she accompanies him to those visits as well, and literally holds her breath until the doctor declares him fit. Then she smiles and reddens as if she's been paid a personal compliment, declared a great beauty or something like her beloved Sharmila Tagore! For Amma, dutifulness is the only expression of love.

I took care of Atal from the moment he was born. For a few years, Amma was proud of me. I was seven when she called me, little Amma. But as he grew older and more precocious, I preferred to make my baby brother a friend and co-conspirator. It was simply more fun! And over the years, I went from *little Amma* to *the little troublemaker*, and *the little toofaan* (storm) and when she ran out of names, I was simply that little ... Ishhhh!

At the end of the day, my mother enjoyed joining Babuji in the living room, dragging her knitting behind her to the couch, where they sat side by side confabulating over the day's events. Until I came in and sat between them with a book or a question. And then, he was no longer hers. He encouraged me to read, to dream, to think beyond the boundaries of home and homeland. We spent hours, playing word games or watching the geography channel. Using up time, he could've spent with his wife.

She must've resented it, at some level. She was increasingly taciturn with me. To get away from her, I dove deeper into my books, pointedly neglecting the stupid little chores she assigned, implying she could easily take care of them herself or ask one of the maids. She grew angrier. It was a spiteful circle.

I was twelve and beginning to be alarmed about the changes in my body. I would not go to Amma, fearful perhaps that as with everything that went wrong, she might somehow make it my fault, that I was leaking blood or growing breasts.

What was worse, boys, whom I'd known all my life, kicked their butts in football and hockey, now made me stutter and sweat in a most perplexing fashion. And just when I thought things couldn't possibly get ghastlier, my face started to break out. One unsightly pimple invited another and soon my forehead became the go-to place for every blackhead, boil and pustule that ever hoped to thrive.

Amma dealt with my ugliness efficiently. She gave me something for stomach cramps, introduced me to deodorants, took me bra shopping without a murmur. I was relieved and impressed, even though I never could say thanks!

But, at some point, she got tired of my endlessly awkward adolescence. My refusal to shed my caterpillar skin and turn into the butterfly of her dreams was beginning to wear her patience thin.

I would feel her eyes on me sometimes, and I could swear I knew what she was thinking ... why can't you be skinny, feminine, light-skinned?

I hardened myself against her scrutiny and focused on schoolwork. Babuji was thrilled. He told me, once, that I was his greatest accomplishment. And despite Amma, I excelled at everything I touched. Almost.

"When you and Khushi arrived at our doorstep, Auntie Maya, I have to admit, I was ambivalent. I desperately needed a friend. A sister, who would draw Amma's negative attention away from me."

But the moment, Khushi, resplendent as the sun, stepped out of the cab, I saw the way Amma's eyes lit up. As if the clouds had parted and the skies would never darken again. I bet she even saw turtle doves and a rainbow where there wasn't any. She never looked at me like that.

I made it a sport of belittling Amma, not so much with words but with meaningful little snorts, sniggers, eyerolls. I knew it hurt and upset her. And each time she came down the stairs with one hand on the balustrade and the other tucked lovingly under Khushi's arm, I would goad Khushi as well.

"Having a nice day, Khushi? Done reading The Love Angel? What's next? The Love Goddess?"

And smile with satisfaction when she turned a deep shade of red.

I was horrid to her. To them both. But she made me so angry, you see. My Amma. Why was she giving Khushi my share of attention? Because I was, I am, a darkie?

"But I did, I do look up to you, Auntie Maya, you know that! I was smitten by your grace, your elegance, your world-weary air as you sat on the terrace, a cigarette between your fingers, smoke curling out of your mouth in composed, leisurely circles. You brought glamour into our lives. A flavour of foreign, uncharted territories."

"I emulated your style, as best I could, and made it a point to suggest that Amma too, have her hair trimmed, or her eyebrows plucked and her chin hair waxed, like auntie Maya. I wanted to pay her back for every second she spent extolling my cousin's virtues, every moment she spent planning to entertain her, take her out shopping and find her a husband. Khushi was her project du jour, filling her days with purpose and excitement."

And I, I was the unhappy outcome of a botched experiment.

Ironical, that it still hurts so much, considering, that until

203

Khushi came along, I never really wanted my mother's infuriating attention, and made it quite clear to her, on more than one occasion. But still.

Just before mid-terms, I caught a movie with my friends – Notting Hill.

When I came out of the movie, I felt strange. My knees kept buckling. My body did not feel like my own. I was restless. Afraid to touch my own skin. Soon after, perhaps that same day, I caught Khushi in her room, doing something, uh ... personal ... you know touching herself. It was the first time I became aware of my body in a different way. My nascent sensuality.

When Bali came by to view Khushi like an Open House, I was still recovering from Hugh Grant's kisses (in my dreams, of course). I saw him, and my heart lurched, although I told myself, he was no Hugh Grant, I hated his silly moustache, and good luck to my cousin, if this was who she wanted.

He proposed marriage, as we all know. Khushi was delighted to be a fiancé and looked positively radiant. Even Atal, my loyal cheetah, was enamoured by her shining eyes, her clear skin. And Amma smiled and smiled and quite forgot to ask me about my exams, or put a piece of coconut, for luck, in my lunch box or worry about the state of my hair. I began feeling invisible. Like one of those ladies in burkhas, who could be anyone or no one.

One day, I found Khushi and Bali kissing in a dark corner of the hallway, where they thought they were alone. They were kissing and making out, quite audibly. I'm afraid, my hormones, so far in check, went quite amok.

Sometimes I found Bali eyeing me on his impromptu lunch visits, like a tasty piece of meat. I knew enough to be offended. But I was not. Instead, I encouraged him, leaning closer to him, making sidebars, pointedly leaving Khushi out of the conversation. He said something mildly flirtatious. I could see he was testing the waters. I laughed maniacally. He amused me. I decided to make myself equally amusing. Together, we made Khushi uncomfortable.

Amma waddled in with trays of food for everyone, scolds and platitudes for me. Somehow, her snooping made it more exciting.

I started looking forward to Bali's visits.

I was beginning to enjoy myself in a novel, terrifying way.

One day he rang the doorbell, accompanied by his nephew, a credulous looking boy, nearer my age. Amma didn't seem to mind, at least, not at first. After all, Bali was now family. And by extension, so was his nephew, Bobby Mehta.

Letting his nephew, now as smitten by Khushi as the rest of the world, strike a conversation with her and keep her occupied, Bali became bolder, openly insolent with me. I matched him, smirk for smirk and naughtiness for naughtiness, noting the way he reared back like a horse, assessing his next move. I knew there would be a next move.

We began seeing each other, secretly.

I told myself, the fact that I was spending time with Bali had nothing to do with Khushi and their relationship. They were to be married. That much was certain. I had no desire to fall in love with him and walk off into the sunset. I was simply widening my network of friends. I was simply punishing Amma for choosing Khushi.

Even so, I found myself avoiding my cousin, scheduling my schoolwork and activities and even my mealtimes in such a way that I did not have to see her. 'Oh, what a tangled web we weave when first we practice to deceive.' Isn't that from one of Walter Scott's poems?

Bali couldn't keep his hands off Khushi. Partly, because she was so beautiful, but mostly because, despite her appeals to maintain a distance, he saw the way she looked at him. I think it thrilled him. He couldn't get enough of her swooning, straight-out-of-a-chick lit longing. While his eyes strayed to where I sat, his hands, almost on their own accord, strayed to her hair, brushed her arm, held her by the waist and manoeuvred her behind walls, behind doorways, behind the bamboo partitions of restaurants, where he pressed his lips to her lips, his body to hers.

At first, I was shocked and fascinated. Like a child happening upon her parents in the bedroom. Then, I felt a stab of envy, even hatred for my cousin. I wished her out of my life.

I wanted her fiancé to want me in that same breathless way. I wanted to win.

I rang his doorbell. That first time, Bali met me at the door, whisked me out, and said, it was inappropriate. Inappropriate! This coming from a man who invented 'inappropriate.'

I pressed my lips to his, told him I wanted our relationship to move to the next level.

"But you are a child," he muttered, almost afraid.

I pushed his lips open with my thumb and forefinger and invited myself in. "Kiss me, the way you kiss her," I whispered.

"I am telling you all this, Auntie Maya, so you know, it was not all Bali's doing."

"I did this. To Khushi. Had I known then, what I know now, perhaps she might be alive."

"Have you ever made mistakes Auntie Maya? I mean, the kind that makes you want to simply disappear? Vanish out of the minds of those who love you, like a bad smell expunged by bleach and replaced with something flawless and uncontaminated? Like incense?"

I didn't disappear. In fact, I continued to revel in my mistake.

"If you call me, I will come," I said to Bali once and so he began to call me, and use me with the zeal and cunning of a seasoned player.

I met him after school, slid into his backseat, my school skirt tenting my thighs, the space between my legs rank smelling with heat and craving. He didn't seem to care how I looked. Or smelled.

I met him in the lavatory of a movie theatre, leaving Amma sitting by herself in the dark and letting him pull down my pants and do unspeakable things. We were caught in the act by a horrible old doorman. Bali had to bribe him to keep him from making a scene. As I ran out of the loo, I heard the old goon smack his lips in a most obscene fashion and called me names I cannot say out loud.

I took a train and a local bus to meet him in town. He pulled me into an empty church and touched me in ways I had never been touched before and I took his heavy groping, his ropy kisses and sibilant breathing, for tokens of love.

There were times, Bali asked me to wear high heels; examined me closely before we went to an adults-only club. He gifted me with lipsticks and cheek colour and drew on my face himself so that I could pass for an eighteen-year-old. I asked him if he thought I should stuff my bra. "No, you are stuffed just right, in that department," he leered.

One day, I did not recognize the face that stared back at me, in the ladies' room mirror. It was unnerving. Before I got home, I made him stop at a Pizza Hut for some comfort food. I washed off the makeup and looked carefully in the mirror again. Despite my clean face, I felt altered. Once home, I had to pull the stuffing out of an old teddy, hide my make-up in there and sew it back on again. It looked weird, so I pushed it out of sight behind other animals. No secret was safe from Amma.

Suddenly Bali was everywhere. His cigarette breath tickled my throat. His musky smell inhabited my clothes. His biting humour infected my mood. His voice over the phone made my heart thump with fear and excitement. My eyes became huge. It was like being on a steady diet of mood-altering pills. So, this is how it must be with Khushi, I thought. And I felt almost sorry for her.

"I tried being nicer to my cousin, from then on, Auntie Maya. And she, because she was inherently kind, did not remind me of my many jibes and my toxic insults, and forgave me easily."

One rainy morning, he invited me to a picnic. It was a public holiday. Bali had reserved a little love suite, (his words, not mine) in the heart of the woods. It was a beautiful drive. I could hear the sound of the waves in the distance, sweet, low, almost lyrical. Birds cooed softly, their tentative mating song.

The wind held the pines in sway, like a snake charmer its prey.

"Wait here," Bali said when we got to the resort.

He went in and collected our room key. I guess he didn't want the staff to see me.

We undressed.

"I was so nervous. I took a deep breath, shut my eyes, and asked him to play some music. That was the first time we really went 'all the way', Auntie Maya."

I thought I heard a sound outside – a murmur of leaves and wind and footsteps falling lightly, which made me more tense. Someone was spying on us, I thought. But I couldn't be sure. I couldn't raise myself to check, in my post-coital haze.

When it was over, I lay back feeling used up and a little sad. I was stretched out on the bed, he was on the recliner, his legs spread out, fingering the fur on his chest. I wished he would put some clothes on. Then he headed to the bathroom. There was something slightly repelling, simian like about him, the way he walked, the way he yawned and scratched and pulled at his member as if he was quite alone.

I quite forgot about the spy at the window – if there even was one.

I took a nap. When I opened my eyes, Bali had his undershirt and his pants back on. He looked freshly showered. Much better, I thought. Hoping to recapture the magic of the morning drive, I whispered, "How much do you love me?"

He laughed. "Love? You are such a baby."

I can still hear him laughing.

By the time we returned, the city was drowning in rain. And I, in humiliation. Add to that, the burden of guilt, as I saw Khushi, day after day, turning into a wraith right before my eyes.

I needed to make things right. There was only one person in the world who I could talk to about my part in Khushi's unhappiness. Of course, the underlying hope was that he would, with his unconditional love and his strong voice of reason, absolve me of blame – I mean, my father, of course.

Babuji was away. He returned from his trip only to pass out in the living room, giving Amma the fright of her life. She put him to bed straight away and wouldn't let anyone near him. I stood in the back of the room shrouded in misery, as his body raged with Dengue fever and his mind succumbed to terror. I watched him toss and turn and call out in sleep, his voice shaking with dread. Even after the fever broke, there were days he could barely raise his head, he was so weak. Besides, Amma was always hovering over him with cold compresses and tepid soup, in her assumed role of part angel, part nurse. I left. There was no one else who could save me from myself.

Bali and I continued to see each other whenever we could. But his laughter, so openly derisive, right after we made love in the woods, still rang in my ears and made me cringe. At some point, we behaved almost like acquaintances despite the callisthenics in bed. The clever sidebars and the volleying back and forth that put a zing in our relationship slowed down, then petered out completely.

One day Amma asked that I go up to Khushi's room. Khushi

had a gash on her forehead and looked pale as a ghost.

The next few weeks were strange. I was told the engagement might be off. And then I heard that it wasn't. There was some misunderstanding.

I never discussed Khushi with Bali. I didn't think it was my place.

Of course, he noticed my lukewarm kisses, my reluctance to bury my face in his starched white shirt and breathe the musky maleness of him, the fact that I no longer looked dreamily into his eyes and say 'I am getting drunk' – and other such nonsense. He is not a dummy. But he did not do anything to revive what I imagined we had, either, and it confirmed what I already knew and had seen often enough – that he was a narcissist, a misogynist and a bully.

One afternoon, I simply forgot to keep my date with him. He didn't call to ask me why. And, just like that, it was over.

By the time my birthday rolled around, I was my old self again.

Cheetah, who I knew was upset with me for some real or imagined wrong, called a truce for the day. My little brother is like a piece of my heart, Auntie Maya – and when he hurts, my heart hurts more. You were there for my party, of course. How lovely you looked, content, imperturbable as always.

Bali was invited too, naturally. Amma eyed him with barely concealed mistrust, (how far the gods had fallen) but we were comfortable enough, Bali and I, and laughed together with impersonal sincerity.

Khushi did not come down to dinner. I saw Amma's eyes flicker with unease. I too felt a faint misgiving, but easily ignored it. It was my day after all, and I did not want to cast a shadow on it.

Something happened to Khushi that evening, of that, I am sure. She locked herself in her room like Sleeping Beauty and did not come down again for days, and when she did, she looked at us as if from a great distance, her vision clouded by atmospheric storms.

Amma spent her time, almost exclusively with Khushi, and shared her fears with Babuji. Atal tried to amuse her in his own sweet way and I ... well, I simply kept out of her hair.

With my sordid little affair behind me, I slept with an easy conscience. How wonderful it was, to not have to lie to my girlfriends, or Amma, and skulk around with a man nearly twice my age. What a tremendous relief to wake up feeling not cheap, or tawdry, and embroiled in a mediocre Lara and Victor Ippolitovich relationship and to know I deserve better. How delicious, to simply hang out in the library in pigtails and a frumpy skirt or share a double scoop of ice cream with a boy pal or rediscover the joys of a sweaty game of field hockey with girls my own age! I shed the sordid portion of my past like excess baggage and felt lighter than air. Revitalized!

Best of all, I no longer felt responsible for Khushi and her ongoing despondency. To be honest, it made me impatient, this role she had immersed herself in – a damsel in distress, forever in need of saving. She was, after all, a guest in our house and, I would think an unwritten rule of protocol is to exchange pleasantries with the host, show some gratitude, give them the gift of a smile! Instead, she chose despair. Wilted without explanation, like a spray of daffodils replete with water and light, wanting for nothing. And my poor, befuddled Amma with her bad back and creaky legs, forever doubling and redoubling her efforts to make her husband's side of the family comfortable. Had Amma paid me a quarter of the attention she paid Khushi, a tenth of it, I would have been overjoyed!

"I'm sorry, but Khushi was like the sun. All she ever had to do in order to warm the lives of those orbiting around her, was to just be."

"She couldn't even manage that ..."

"I was in the throes of a terrible dream when I heard the screaming. My mind, still in a shambolic state, refused to process what I saw, even though I heard myself say: There's a puppet hanging from the ceiling fan – Oh, it's Khushi!"

It was when I saw the look on Atal's face that I realized this was no hallucination. I wanted to shunt him out of the room, hide him from the ghastly apparition that was his cousin. But he pointed a finger at me, "It was you, your fault." He said, his voice thin and squeaky, his eyes unflinching.

I believed him. And judging by the blow that fell on my hip, so did Babuji – that god-fearing, intrinsically loving man.

"It occurred to me, at last, that Khushi had known all along, Bali was cheating on her. With me. How could she have not?"

"Khushi did not take her own life. My actions led to her demise."

"And what I want to say to you, Auntie Maya is that I am so, so sorry. Your loss is huge, I know that well, but I too have lost a sister. I did love her. I know this now. I wish I had known this before."

"I regret my cruelty. My selfishness. I admit that the anger I felt for her was simply a way of coping with my lack of esteem. I regret what we, our family have become – little islands unto ourselves, windless, and inaccessible."

"Babuji will not forgive me. I hope you can. Please say, you can."

Because I am suffocating under the weight of our collective guilt. And if I could disappear, I would. Just like Khushi.

Mumbai

The watchman, the maid and the memsahib.

Twenty-Seven

"**I** wanted to disappear from that house of horrors, as fast as my legs could carry me," the watchman confided to Radha, his voice heavy with fear and cigarette smoke.

"She hung there like a doll, Khushi, but the expression on her face was devilish. Simply devilish!" He crossed himself, then folded his hands and bowed prayerfully, and finally prostrated himself on the floor, hoping to appease every god he could think of - Hindu, Moslem, and Christian – all surely, regarding him with fire and brimstone from their heavenly abode.

"So, what happens next?" A sullen Radha asked her part-time lover. "Do we get nothing? All that time spent spying on the household, so we would have enough dirt when we blackmail them into returning what they took from me? My livelihood?" Then, seeing the expression on his face, she lifted her face heavenward and with a passion worthy of Scarlett O'Hara, exclaimed, "As Laxmi is my witness, I will not be left penniless!"

Then Gopi, invoking deities of the Hindu pantheon, shrieked, "Don't smite me dead, O Shiva!"

O Kali! O Yama! She wants to make money off the deceased girl, not me, never me," and still in his pyjamas, dashed out of his shanty, past the No. 83 bus stop and over the bridge, with a vague idea of crossing the train tracks, to get over the other side, as far away as possible from his temptress. But the watchman caught his foot on the railroad track and met the wrath of an oncoming train, instead.

Twenty-Eight

Unfazed by her idiot lover's departure, following her train of thought to a successful conclusion, Radha stepped out of the shanty, glancing back once at the Solanki residence, now cloaked in darkness.

That night, she slept fitfully for a few hours, felt the need to urinate three times, then smoked a bidi to pass the time until dawn.

At 8 a.m. she was ringing Maya memsahib's doorbell. Better to catch her early, before she dashed off to work, rather than waylay her at the end of the day. Radha knew, from her lengthy period of spying, Maya did not keep regular hours and was often out all night.

Not that much different from my life, except she has better clients, Radha smirked.

Maya heard the doorbell and ignored it. She hadn't slept in a week, subsisted on stale potato chips and cigarettes, and found herself shaking with nervousness and nausea.

The doorbell rang again.

"Who the f***?" She muttered. No one was expecting her at work. She had given notice to the maid and told the watchman she wanted no milk, no groceries, and no newspaper delivered to her door.

She opened the door. "Who the hell are you?" She barked.

"I am Radha, previously the maid, and I have a story for you."

"The Solankis' maid, right? Please go away. I feel unwell."

But Radha slid past Maya, went into the living room and lowered herself on the granite floor, where she squatted as if about to relieve herself. "Sit, memsahib," she patted the sofa.

Maya, sighing in disgust, heard Radha out.

"I slept with Bali half a dozen times. He gave me abortion money." Radha said, without wasting breath on niceties.

"So?"

Radha blinked. "I also saw Miss Sami in his car – Bali's – several times. He took her to clubs. I am sure of it. The watchman knows all about it, as well."

Maya sat rigid as a doll, her eyes so far in the distance, Radha wondered if she had taken off for the spirit world.

"Again, why are you telling me this?" Maya gritted her teeth.

"And I saw him come to your flat, many times. And not leave, until morning."

Still no expression on Maya's face – not a flicker of anger. Not a raised brow. Not even a pulse, signalling distress.

"Are you done? Khushi is gone. Nobody cares about any of this. Do you not get it? Now, if you have no more stories about Bali and his fucking adventures, with me or with anybody else, you can leave."

Radha, previously the Solanki maid, clenched her fists for courage.

"The watchman told me, Bali refused to marry Miss Khushi. He called her a two-timing tart."

"Why are you here? What is it that you want from me? Tell me!" Maya banged a fist on the side table.

"Cash!" Radha said, with spirit. "Or I will tell the press your daughter took her life because of all these ..."

She paused, desperate for a mot juste.

"The press! And they will believe you? A two-bit whore?"

Radha gulped. It occurred to her, that things were not going the way she had imagined. The memsahib was right. Who would believe her? Who would even give her the time of day?

She made one, last-ditch effort.

"We could blackmail Bali and his family. The three of us. Maid, watchman and memsahib. Then they will surely pay us! They deserve to suffer. Look what he did to your daughter."

"Bali is in a hospital bed. Beaten, almost dead. Go now, you stupid, stupid girl before I smash your little brain with ... this" – she held a corporate recognition award she had received that same year, high in her hand – "and empty you on the street like a piece of trash."

The obelisk-shaped tower tapered to a sharp point and appeared to have a very heavy base.

Radha felt the tip of the tower press against her neck, then inch higher. She rose, backed out of the apartment and shut the door behind her.

Maya double-locked the door and went into the bathroom where she retched and retched and finally flushed the non-existent splash of sputum.

Wiping her face with a warm towel, she thought ... So ... *Sami ... He got her too, the randy little punk.*

She made up her mind to see Sami and show her the newspaper clipping about Bali and perhaps get her version of the facts.

218

Twenty-Nine

"**I** guess, she's upstairs, in her room, if you must see her again," Kamla muttered tiredly.

Maya nodded. "Can I have a cup of tea, Kamla, before I go up to Sami?"

"Of course. Where are my manners. We can sit in the kitchen."

Kamla set the tea things out and busied herself emptying sweet and salty snacks into delicate silver bowls.

Maya eyed her sister-in-law with resentment. The dark circles under her eyes, the wispy hair more grey than black, the white cotton sari swathed around her body like a rumpled sheet, clearly the woman was crying for help. Maya did not want to condole with her sister-in-law anymore. She was not the one who lost a daughter. Besides, Maya felt she had done her bit. It was time Kamla moved on.

Maya had stayed on at the Solanki residence for a few months after her daughter's passing. She had slept on Khushi's bed, bathed in Khushi's bathroom, hung her clothes in Khushi's closet. She had cried desperately, endlessly – not like a mother but like a child crying over a broken dolly, a baby gone useless.

One day she went down to the kitchen and came upon Kamla, hunched over a cup of tea. She had forgotten to add milk and appeared to be watching the muddy brew with some confusion.

Maya took the ice-cold cup of tea out of her ice-cold hands and poured it down the sink. She heated some milk, added a tinge of turmeric and a generous amount of sugar and placed a mugful in front of Kamla. "Have it."

Kamla looked at the proffered drink. Blinked.

"Look, I'm having some too." Maya took a sip of the nourishing beverage.

Kamla drank her milk. When she was done, she wiped her mouth with the back of her hand.

"What now?" She asked Maya, awaiting direction.

Maya took her in her arms.

After she was done crying, done washing her face with cold water and wiping it with the ends of her sari, Kamla said in a choked voice, "You put her in my care. I let you down."

"You were more a mother to her than I could ever be, Kamla. I want you to remember that always, because, I will never say it again."

With that she left her, to find Sri.

Babuji was in the study, journaling. When Maya came in, he stood up and folded his hands in a formal gesture that took them both by surprise.

"Sri."

She came around the desk and put her arms around him.

The sibs held each other and it was not clear who needed comforting, and who was the older of the two.

"Your daughter. I should have ..."

"Not you, Sri." She said, holding his face in her hands, "It was I who should have."

Kamla had the tea ready. "Where would you like to sit?"

"Right here, is fine." They ate and drank in silence.

"Where are the servants, Kamla? It's so quiet here." Kamla looked into the distance.

"I fired them. I can manage on my own. I don't have the energy to ..." Her voice trailed off.

Maya nodded, patted her sister in-law's back and went up to Sami's room.

Sami was at her desk, listening to something, her headphones over her ears. She saw Maya and greeted her warmly.

What was troubling, thought Maya, was that the girl, like any teenager in a relationship with an older man, had blamed herself and was convinced she had lost her moral compass. What if, a chill ran down Maya's spine, what if Sami, still suffering from post-traumatic stress, trapped in the quicksand of guilt, and remorse, did something drastic? Just like Khushi.

"Thank you for being so upfront with me, the other day. I've always appreciated that quality in you."

Sami's eyes glistened.

"Will you do a couple of things for me Sami? For the sake of what I once meant to you, and perhaps still do?

Sami nodded eagerly. "Anything. Anything."

"I noticed, on my way in, that Atal was up on a tree, staring without his binoculars, at nothing discernible, as far as I could tell. He looks, quite frankly, as if he hasn't bathed in days and seems a little lost. Can you, the person he loves more than anyone in the world, take more care of him? He's still not too old for some rituals – tuck him into bed at night, take him, for an occasional ice cream. Read him a book, perhaps?"

Sami snivelled into her kerchief.

"Atal blames me. He hates me."

"Atal is confused. He is a child. So, will you do it?" Auntie Maya asked gently.

"Yes. What's the other thing?"

"You are so talented. You have so much curiosity. You should get as far away as possible from all this sadness. Would you like to study abroad, as I did? I will help you."

"I very much would. It's just ..."

"What?"

"I can't help thinking, Auntie Maya, here I am, making plans ... the bright lights of New York beckoning me into the future and all that, when really, shouldn't I be punished in some way ...?"

Maya eyed her niece and saw that it was not self-pity, nor was it a narcissistic need to draw attention away from Khushi. She was honestly troubled.

"Sami, listen to me well, because every word of it is true. Khushi's troubles had less to do with you than you think. I know this for a fact." Then taking a deep breath, she went on, "We all have our secrets. I have mine. So, does your Amma and Sri – yes, trust me – and so did Khushi. You may never learn of my mistakes. Of the crimes I committed, albeit unintentionally, against my own child – It would serve no purpose. Just don't, please don't carry more than your share of the burden, my darling child." She paused to take her niece's hands in her own.

A rush of fresh air made the curtains on Sami's window billow like Victorian skirts.

"Okay!" Sami finally said, softly.

Then, she threw the window open letting sunlight fill the walls, her pillow, the stuffed animals on the shelf, with pointillistic dabs and flickers.

"Okay!" She bounded across the room, to hug and squeeze her aunt.

"I will go abroad if you will help me. You are the best, Auntie Maya."

Maya nodded, hugged her back. "Then, it's done."

They sat side by side with their own thoughts. A mother looking back, a child looking forward.

New York-Mumbai

Semper deinceps.

Thirty

On the drive home from the 100-year-old-man's place, Martin looked at his bride, wet-eyed and happy.

What is her story? He wondered. What the heck is her story?

But there was no time to wonder because Patrick was waiting on the front stoop, armed with roller skates, a mint chocolate chip ice-cream cone and a brand-new backpack. It appeared, his mother had an appointment she absolutely had to keep – despite the fact that it was Sunday – and had handled the situation with her customary bribe first, apologize later, strategy.

For Patrick's sake, Martin tried to look complacent, he didn't want his son to think he was not welcome, even though his honeymoon – minimoon really, was not quite over. He got off the car and sauntered over to his son.

"Sweetheart, you are home. Did Mama let you wait here all by yourself?"

"Nope. Grandma brought me."

"Where is she?"

"She went into the house with her key. 'Cos, she had to use the bathroom and also leave a surprise casserole for you ... Oops!" Patrick clamped a hand over his mouth.

"That's okay, Cheetah, we'll pretend we didn't hear the last bit,"

Sami winked.

"Who's Cheetah?"

"What?"

"You called me Cheetah. I'm Patrick."

"I ... I know ... I ..." Sami looked as white as a sheet.

"It's in fun. Besides, a cheetah is one of the smartest, fastest animals on the planet." Martin went on all fours, held his hands over his head and pretended to lock horns with his son.

Patrick shrieked with delight.

Sami collected herself and started towards the house, just as Lynn was getting out the front door.

"Hello, darling. I apologize for barging in, but Barbara dropped Patrick over and today is Bingo night at the *Senior Center*. It's my turn to ..."

"No worries, Lynn, you needn't explain," Sami interrupted gently.

"Hi, Mom," Martin waved.

"Martin." Lynn stepped forward, then turned her head to look at Sami again.

"Can I just say, you look wonderful in that costume – I mean – outfit. Like a princess. Honestly."

"Thank you. I'll just go in and freshen up ..."

"Sami, wait!"

"Yes?"

"There was a call for you, while I was putting away a casserole for you two lovebirds. I answered the phone, without thinking. I hope that was okay?

"That's quite alright. Who was it?"

"Uh. I've written her name and number down. It's on your centre island ... she said auntie Maya, I think?"

Sami's heart dropped.

"Why, whatever is the matter, Sami? You look like you've seen a ghost!"

Martin, alerted by the alarm in Lynn's voice, made it to his wife's side in three long strides. He put his arm around Sami.

"Let's go inside. We'll sort it out. Whatever it is."

Thirty-One

Six years and counting thought Sami. Yes. Perhaps it was time to sort it all out.

Sami poured herself a gin and tonic. Something she had never done before and often teased Martin about. "Why do men feel the need to moisten their mouths, at the slightest hint of stress?"

But now she did. Need to moisten her mouth, that is. Her salivary glands seemed to have dried up so completely, the word arid came to mind.

She finished her drink. Then resolutely, looked at the number Lynn had scribbled on a stickie.

"It's local," Martin said, hugging her from the back, resting his chin on her shoulder.

Sami nodded. "She is here. I have to go to her."

"Why? You could invite her over for a drink. We even have gin," he teased.

Sami, about to say something, closed her mouth, looking uncomfortable.

"Or not," Martin said, seeing the expression on his wife's face.

"Let me call her first, we'll see," she muttered and walked across the kitchen to the deck.

Martin, with supreme delicacy, left the room, saying something about getting Patrick ready for bed.

The woman who answered the knock was not the sunny sophisticate she remembered but one who had weathered many a long winter. Maya's face and neck were creased with lines, the veins in her hands popped in a rather startling fashion and her elbows looked dry and withered, but the expression in those winsome eyes remained the same – Cool and inscrutable. And the way she held herself, so proud and erect, Sami was sure she could still bring any man down a peg or two.

"Auntie Maya!" Sami had trouble speaking, trouble breathing.

Maya took her face in her hands, kissed her head, her chin, both her cheeks.

"Let me look at you," she said, at last, holding her at arm's length, her voice gruff with emotion.

Sami allowed herself to be appraised then shied away, touched and almost embarrassed by the love in her aunt's eyes.

"I've ordered us a little something," auntie Maya said when they sat down. "But we can always go down to the restaurant, if you like."

"No. I'd rather be here."

There was silence for a minute or two. But it was not a tear-laden silence. Rather, it was a moment of appreciation. A moment of thanksgiving.

Then auntie Maya said, "I will not waste time with admonitions and complaints, Sami. I am here for a specific reason. But first, tell me everything that's been going on with you. Starting from that awkward moment at the airport when we barely had time to say goodbye, until now." She smiled.

Sami smiled back uncertainly.

"Go on!" Auntie Maya prodded.

Then Sami, as once before, opened up like a book. She spoke to auntie Maya about how the minute she found herself in the air, she was overcome with rivalling emotions – so happy to be getting away, so equally heartbroken that they let her go. To be precise, that Babuji let her go, without a word. And Amma had not come to the door, claiming she hated goodbyes, could not handle them. And even Atal watched her leave from atop his tree and only when she was bundled into the cab, her suitcases struggling to detach themselves, chained as they were to the roof rack, that she saw him slide down like a monkey and chase the cab, but she, in a fit of spite, did not turn her head around to wave back.

In New York, she was met by a relative, who spoke with an accent and treated her with disdain. We do things differently here he kept saying, implying they did everything bigger, better, faster than people at home.

She thought he was ridiculous in his flared pants and sneakers. His wife, a medical doctor, worked long hours and barely had time to microwave a meal, and his two obnoxious brats watched too much TV and were so limited in every way it boggled the mind.

A week later, she moved to university housing and vowed she would rather slit her wrists than meet them again.

She kept her head down, busied herself with her books. Did well.

Babuji sent her tuition fees directly to the university and thus avoided communicating with her. In the evenings, she walked up and down Lexington Avenue, where she usually ate a meal in one of the hole-in-the-wall restaurants, or Times Square or the West Village to get a glimpse of other people, other lives.

Then she went home, checked her mailbox and dreamt night after night, of food – tubs, trays and woks of – orangey slurries speckled with greenish bits of chicken and fish, lamb and pork that she devoured with the appetite of a caged and starving animal. She rose from sleep feeling full and nauseous, and with a pain between her eyes that drove her to the toilet where she puked the illusory repast until she dry-heaved.

In her fourth year, she met the hundred-year-old man. He lived in the apartment below hers. He was the first friend she ever made. And the only one. His caretaker, Mrs Mistry taught Sami a thing or two about cooking, and sewing a button and so on.

She was temping at a law firm, to make some extra money, Sami said, colouring slightly, when she met Martin. He was a criminal lawyer with an impressive caseload of pro bono cases. At least, she was impressed.

He was divorced. Had a little boy. They started seeing each other. Martin encouraged her to study further, get her MSW. So, she did. She was now married, trying to be a good step-mommy to Patrick and held a decent job – gratifying. And someday, when she could make sense of it all, she hoped to write her story. The end. Sami shrugged.

Auntie Maya did not interrupt once, poring over her every word with flattering intensity.

There was a small silence after Sami was done speaking, pleasant and almost sad, like evening rain.

"Hundred-year-old-man? Really?" Auntie Maya, finally said, arching her neatly plucked brows.

"Yes. He is my guiding light. I have moved jobs, moved out of the neighbourhood, since I first met him, but each time I back my car out of my driveway, it noses towards him. I will introduce you. He is a real treasure."

"I would like that. I would like to meet the one person in the world you chose to call your friend in so many years."

Sami did not respond for a while.

Then she said, her eyes on the floor, "I did not want for anything when I got here. At least, not at first.

I had school. Books. Room and board. So much to absorb. So much to forget.

But then the memories started building, piling one on top of another. I had nowhere to unload. When I met the hundred-year-old man in his wheelchair, his eyes watery but alert, his cheeks the colour of red apples, I was filled with nostalgia for I do not know what or whom.

Or perhaps, it was for that feeling of absolute peace that comes from being in the one place, where you can take a break from judgements. Where your face is known, your clothing goes unnoticed, and your words received with open arms.

And you may be settled quietly in your own room with your door shut, but you know, seated on a rocker, a shawl around his shoulders, somewhere close by there is the rosy-cheeked householder, should you need him – a night light to ease your fears, a benediction that glows in your heart."

"I'm glad you met. I'm glad you have him." Auntie Maya said.

Then it was Sami's turn.

"Auntie Maya, you said you were here for a specific reason?"

Auntie Maya nodded. "Yes."

Then putting a thumb under Sami's chin, tilted it upward so that they were at eye level, she said, "I am here to take you home. Your parents need you."

Sami swallowed.

"Are they all right? Babuji?" She whispered.

"As well as they can be, under the circumstances."

"What circumstances, auntie Maya? I mean, other than ...

233

Khushi?"

"And is there any other loss they need to suffer before you will grace them with your presence?"

Sami felt her eyes prickle.

"No. No. Of course not," she burst into tears. "I'm sorry."

Auntie Maya's hands shook. She fought for composure, the blankness of her face when in repose, now marred with strain.

"That's alright. My fault. I admit I have become quite touchy of late."

"I have been wanting to come home for a very long time," Sami said, softly. It's all I ever think of. My thoughts of home blur everything I see, like a page, handwritten on both sides.

The tastes, the smells, the dialects of home are beginning to affect me in hallucinatory ways. Nothing here seems real. I am simply biding my time, still at the airport, still waiting for Babuji to appear... and either permit me to leave or turn me around and take me home. I still don't know which.

"Then why haven't you come?"

"Because ... Why didn't they ever ask me to? Why have they forgotten me?"

Auntie Maya was silent. There were so many ways to respond to her niece. At last, she decided to simply side-step the question.

"You mustn't cry, Sami. How does that help?" She said, covering Sami's hand with her own. After a few moments, almost speaking to herself, she said softly,

"It is my belief that after Khushi, they lost all confidence. Years ago, when I first broke it to your father that you were keen on going abroad, he agreed so readily, I too was surprised. I thought he might be a bit more protective of his own child, not want to send her out into the world, all alone, in the face of such a big loss."

"Then he told me, that he and Kamla had made some errors of judgement with Khushi they did not want to repeat with you. They wanted you to be happy. I suppose, giving you carte blanche, to travel, study, run free, was their way of making up for past mistakes. And, let us not forget, your parents have always put your needs above their own, paying for your education, your stay abroad, have they not?"

"Met my needs? Met my needs by distancing me from their lives? Like an achoot?"

Auntie Maya's shoulders slumped. Finally, sighing deeply, she simply asked, "Will you come home, Sami?"

And Sami replied, "Yes," just as simply..

———❦———

"**Y**es," said Martin, simply. "Of course, you must go."

And so, here they were, at the airport lounge, aunt and niece, weighed down with bags, and travel anxiety.

There was a flight delay. Restlessly, auntie Maya, rose from her seat to stretch her legs.

"I'll watch your bag if you want to get coffee, or whatever," Sami said.

"No. Sami, let's go sit there, it's quieter." They moved to a table for two, with a view of the airfield.

Auntie Maya watched the giant machines taxi, lift into the air and become a blur. Inexplicably, her eyes filled.

"What is it, Auntie Maya?" Sami asked, worried.

"Nothing, dear."

"I love you, Auntie," Sami said.

In the sixty-odd years, she had accumulated on the planet, no one had ever said those words to Maya with any real feeling. Not her parents, not Sri, not the father of her child. Not even her child. Perhaps it was her fault – wittingly or unwittingly – she scared love away.

Sami was looking at her, waiting.

Maya took a deep breath.

"Sami, you know, for a long time, I couldn't bear to look at a plane or even a bird in flight. It made me unbearably sad. One moment they were among us, those harbingers of hope, the next they were gone, flown off to unknown parts. And I felt, hopelessly left behind."

"But then, one night, I happened to raise my eyes to the skies and saw a plane twinkle between the stars, and I followed its gliding light for as long as I could before it disappeared into the milky way. And it occurred to me that I was no longer sad. I felt, in fact, proud and happy."

"There goes my Khushi, I thought. There she goes. Blazing new trails with her strong, beautiful light."

Sami nodded, at a loss for words.

"But the thing is Sami," auntie Maya cupped her niece's face with her hands, "After a while, I began seeing your face in the stars – you are my happiness now. My *khushi*."

Sami stared at her aunt, amazed she was the recipient of so much love, shocked that her aunt would admit it.

"But Auntie Maya ... Khushi ... I mean ..."

Auntie Maya placed a finger on her niece's lips.

"Shhh! I don't think of all the misery, but of all the beauty that still remains – Anne Frank." She explained.

"Thank you, Auntie. You've made me so happy." Sami leaned forward for a kiss.

Thirty-Two

"*Khush raho.*" Stay happy, Amma said formally, allowing herself to be hugged. Babuji placed a hand on her head, mussed her hair with affection, then motioned her indoors. Sami stood in the centre of the room surrounded by what seemed to her, a great number of people.

"Where's Atal?" She whispered.

"Fell asleep, waiting," Amma said. "It is a bit late."

She was asked to sit down. A glass of water was thrust into her hands and taken away a moment later.

"Have this instead," Amma said, giving her a glass of mango *lassi*.

She sipped the iced drink gratefully. It was unseasonably warm, even for Mumbai. A coffee table was set before her. Sami, seated like a maharani, although not as comfortably, surveyed the mountain of samosas, toast, fruit, and assorted puddings, perplexed. When she looked down next, there was a cup of tea in her hands, the mango lassi having been whisked off like a pesky relative to parts unknown. And, was she dreaming, or was there music, playing in the background? Loud? In Babuji's presence!

"And how are you? You look wonderful! So pretty! Are you taller?" A familiar-looking woman exclaimed.

Auntie Maya bent down to kiss her. "Patience." She whispered. Then turning to her brother, she said,

"Sri. I have a car waiting. Walk me out."

At the door, he took his sister's arm.

"But why don't you stay? He pleaded.

Maya looked at him perceptively. "She's your daughter, Sri. She's home now. All she wants is her father's attention. Go to her. And send all those women clucking around her, home too, for goodness' sake. Don't they realize how late it is?"

Sami tossed and turned in her old bed. She didn't recognize the sheets, the blanket, the towels Amma had thoughtfully placed, folded neatly, on a chair. But the wallpaper was the same – little baskets of posies against a yellow backdrop. Cheesy, and incredibly comforting. Behind her eyelids throbbed a thousand lights, multitudinous notes of music, Bollywood baring its jarring, complex heart. She checked the time on her phone. 6 a.m.

Amma would be up any minute. Perhaps they could share a quiet cup of tea together. The thought made her head swim - thirty-six hours ago, she was motherless.

Sami padding down the hallway, found herself outside the guestroom. Her heart flapping like a bird, she went in and switched on the lights.

Amma had Khushi's room repainted a hospital white. The bed and the guest chairs, she noted, were not just replaced but also rearranged and centred towards a floating entertainment centre, a weird, modern-day interloper on the wall. There was no trace of Khushi in the room. She checked the wardrobe. Khushi's clothes were gone. There were a couple of skirts, a sari – definitely auntie Maya's. It was her perfume that lingered in the corners, wafted out of the woodwork, not her daughter's sweet lily-of-the-valley scent. She shut the wardrobe.

Her eyes fell on the curtains swooshing and sighing in the morning breeze. Amma had left them alone.

Sami went to the window. If she leaned her head out of the window, Khushi, hearing the doorbell, would've seen the entrant, and if it was her fiancé, surely, she would've run down to get the door? As a matter of fact, Sami remembered seeing her get the door for Bali, catching her breath at the bottom stair, fighting for composure, plenty of times. Sami clutched at the curtain for support. Then, breathing deeply, she let go. Something caught her eye. She lifted the curtain, nearer the seam. It was discoloured and rubbed down cautiously as if someone had tried to spot clean but missed a few squiggles. Sami looked at it closely. Pink nail colour, Khushi's favourite shade.

Bile rose in Sami's throat. Khushi had hung herself with a pink scarf. Quietly, she left the room, shutting the door after her.

How quickly the old routines fall into place. Amma was at the kitchen table, warming her hands on her cup of tea. Eyes shut, she was swaying to the hypnotic rhythm of her morning chant.

I've seen her like this before, my Amma, Sami thought and unaccountably welled up.

Amma opened her eyes. "Sami, what is it Child, could you not sleep?"

"I thought I would have a cup of tea."

"Of course." Amma started to get up.

"No. I'll get it. You finish your prayers, Amma." Sami went past Amma, giving her shoulders a gentle squeeze.

The kettle was still warm and there was enough water for another cup.

"Ah! I was nearly done. He knows what is in my heart, anyway, Sami." Amma smiled, peacefully.

Sami found a mug for her Darjeeling tea and a pack of Marie Biscuits, that made her smile in remembrance.

"Amma, something's bothering me," she said, pulling her chair closer to her mother.

Amma arched her brows.

"You have not been taking care of your health. Babuji says you need to have your cataracts removed. And your knees are giving you way too much trouble. Anyone can see you are in pain. Surgery will make you good as new, Amma!"

"Ishhhh! Surgery. What is the point of putting a new mattress on old bed springs?"

A sudden image of Amma, wide as a mattress, bouncing on old bed springs made Sami cough and splutter.

Amma! Seriously ... Sami tried to pull herself together, choked, and fell into a fit of giggles.

Amma, unsure what was so funny, joined in just the same, and for a few moments, the house resounded with pure, undiluted laughter. Then just as suddenly, she stopped.

"Sami, Amma said, pensively, did you not miss this old 'mattress' who gave you birth?"

"You must know I did, Amma. Every single day."

It was clear, Amma needed more than that. She looked so lost, her scant, wayward hair emphasizing the circles under her eyes, dark clouds that came to stay.

"I have the paisley shawl you gave me for my birthday. I wear it every chance I get. It always makes me feel better, Amma."

Amma nodded. And kept nodding for a long time. Another one of her quirks that Sami noted with fondness.

"And you? Did you not miss me?"

Amma smiled. "What a question. I am your mother. I even made up stories for Atal."

"But you always did that. Make up stories," Sami pouted, feeling a little cheated.

"Yes. But after you left, I told him stories about a little girl who travelled far and away on the wings of a peacock." Amma said, shyly.

Peacocks can't really fly too far, the critic in Sami wanted to say, but she did not. They were Amma's stories. Who was she to question them?

Sami rose and hugged Amma from behind, resting her chin for a moment, on her creased and papery neck. "I need to shower," Sami said.

"Where's Atal?" Sami asked, much later, when she came down for breakfast.

Left for school while she was still in the shower, Amma said, a perplexed look on her face. Sami nodded, without comment.

Sometime during the day, she cornered Babuji alone in his study.

He looked smaller, hunched over his books, grey hair peeking out of his nose, his ears, his chest. His eyes, like Amma's, looked weak and tired from the recounting of countless memories.

"You are avoiding me."

"No. Yes." Babuji glanced at the door, gestured that she shut it.

"I have been preparing a speech, Samar."

He just called me by my full name.

"Speech?"

"I owe you an apology. Those many years ago, at the time of Khushi's passing, I hurt you. And although this does not absolve me, I want you to know, it was unintentional. I would never aim my cane at you, and I just don't understand, cannot explain my impulse to fling it across the room – I am not a violent man. I hope ... I hope I am not ..."

She thought of a paper boat, floundering in the wind.

"Do you forgive me?"

His cheeks are wet.

She took in the room. She had seen these books a thousand times in her mind's eye, caught a whiff of them at the NYC public library, and on the shelves of independent bookstores where she obsessively browsed, and in every hushed corner of the city where bookstores stood like trees of good.

She walked from aisle to aisle, feet tap-tapping on the floor until, "Are you looking for a particular book, Miss?" Asked the shop owner, the librarian, the salesman. Then she found herself staring at them, frozen with uncertainty. No, she wanted to say, it's not a book. It's the feeling of being cocooned in warmth. It's the musty smell of old worlds and familiar stories. It is a perfect, loving sentence leading up to a perfect, dreamless night. Where can I get that?

"Samar?"

"It's fine, Babuji. It wasn't you. It was an occurrence. An anomaly."

Her voice dropped to a whisper,

"I was the one at fault. I ruined all of our lives. I went against everything you taught me."

Babuji shook his head vigorously.

"You were a child! You and Khushi. Two little girls, dreaming of a future, under my protection. Now one is lost for all time and the other ..."

"The other is still here. If you will have me," said, Sami.

She was sitting on his bed with her gift for him, the 'Impossible is Nothing' poster with Muhammed Ali's glove bursting out of the sheet rolled up and propped by her side, when he walked in.

"Cheetah," Sami breathed, wonder in her voice.

"My name is Atal, not Cheetah," he said, his voice adenoidal.

"You've grown!"

"......"

"What have you been up to for the past six years?"

"Seven. Almost seven years. What have you been up to?"

"Hard to say."

"Hard to say, for me too."

"Stop copying me."

"Stop copying me!"

"I missed you too."

"I missed you, three."

His dimple danced with awkward glee.

Her dimple followed, joyfully.

After that, the days tumbled into each other, playfully.

Atal made it easier for her to stay, with his easy banter, showing her, not so much with words as with his sweet ways, that he needed his sister far more than he did his anger.

Of course, there were loose ends that needed tying. Sami recognized this, each time she walked down the hallway, past the guest room where Khushi's spirit still lurked despite the fresh décor, the deodorized air.

To bring up her cousin with Amma would be like performing open-heart surgery for the second time. Amma was not ready. Her guess was, she never would be.

And Babuji. No, Sami thought, remembering the wetness of his cheeks, his face contorted like a child's. Just no.

As always, she reached out to her aunt. "Shall I come over?" Auntie Maya asked eagerly.

"We will have more privacy, at yours. Also, I'd like to see some of my old haunts, along the way. I haven't been out once, since I arrived."

Auntie Maya agreed, readily. "Come around, noon. We will have lunch together."

Driving into town, Sami watched with pensive eyes, her beloved city, every building a reminder of passing time – infirm, down-trodden homes, grasping for a foothold, listening for the death-knell, but also, glass and steel structures emerging like juggernauts out of the rubble of previous dwellings. Soon the city will be completely unrecognisable, existing only in memory, she thought. Until even the memories are gone.

Auntie Maya lived on the 37th floor in a building that towered over Mumbai, like an-America-returned-architect's boast of dazzling glass. On her way up to the 37th floor she thought of her aunt – how she vacillated between anger and grief, and her brave quote from Anne Frank's diary about the beauty that still remains – now etched in Sami's memory. Holding her breath, she knocked on the door.

"I love your apartment, auntie Maya. It's so You!" Sami, exclaimed, quite forgetting her trepidation of just moments before. She admired the clutter of handloom pillows contrasting harmoniously with the dark leather sofas; vibrant Warli art covered the ceiling and a very modern bar filled almost the entire living room.

Auntie Maya settled herself in an armchair framed in polished mahogany and tilted her chin towards its twin.

"Sit. Let me know when you are ready to eat. I have ordered a rather eclectic mix of Rogan josh, *naans*, chicken salad and cucumber sandwiches."

"Perfect! I will have some of everything."

Auntie Maya eyed her with affection.

"Catch me up." She ordered.

Obediently, Sami told her aunt about her conversations with Amma and Babuji, watching her aunt's face closely. She spoke about her reconciliation with Atal and how the mere sight of him still filled her with joy. "He is so beautiful. Like an armful, a truck full of joy!"

Auntie Maya smiled quietly.

"I'm glad, Sami. That's real progress."

Over lunch, Sami teased her about the bar. "You must get really thirsty," she winked.

"The company would use my apartment to entertain international clients. Ply them with the flavours of home while they cooked deals with them, I suppose. All that's over now. I'm not a newsreader anymore. Fortunately, I was able to buy off the flat."

In her customary matter-of-fact manner, she told Sami she had formed India's first support group for survivors of loss.

"This is my fourth year. I am on tour for 123 days a year, on speaking engagements, and so forth. We are now in discussions, to take it further, with a hotline for troubled teens. How does CHOOSE LIFE sound to you?"

Sami nodded, bit her lip.

"It sounds like a wonderful project, Auntie Maya. But you

might need a supporting slogan if you use that name for your hotline. By itself, it may read like an anti-abortion clinic."

Auntie Maya's eyes widened. "Oh, I hadn't thought of that! Thank you, Sami." Sami smiled, pleased with herself.

"You are amazing. I'm so, so proud to be your niece."

Auntie Maya nodded quietly, lost in thought.

"Let's have coffee in the living room, Sami" she said.

When they were settled, she cocked an eyebrow at Sami, "You have something you want to know, yes? That's one of the reasons you are here, today."

Sami was suddenly self-conscious.

"I'm still struggling with guilt, Auntie Maya. And I have so many questions. Something's wrong with the timeline. I mean, my affair with Bali was over quite a few weeks before Khushi took her own life. I'm not even certain she knew about us. Why did they really break up again? My parents know something, but I dare not ask them. What was going on with her?"

And auntie Maya felt compelled to respond.

Shocked and saddened beyond belief, Sami left auntie Maya's apartment, barely feeling the affectionate press of arms, or the peck on her cheek before she quietly shut the door behind her.

On the drive home, she did not let the mid-day traffic muscle its way into her consciousness. She was elsewhere, grappling with mayhem of another kind.

"Khushi was raped. Bali raped her."

Sami shivered at the cold, hard way auntie Maya stated the facts. It could not have been consensual sex, because her daughter was never herself again, Maya said. That much was obvious to the family. Then Khushi found herself pregnant. And Bali refused to marry her. He knew a shotgun wedding would not enhance his, or his family's reputation in any way, shape or form.

Adding insult to injury, he all but accused her of two-timing. The miserable piece of trash! Traumatized as any rape victim, used and humiliated by the man who promised to shelter her from the storms of life, she couldn't find a way out of her shame.

Auntie Maya's lips trembled with suppressed rage. "But how ... who ..." Sami was obviously at a loss for words.

"There was no autopsy - Sri, for the first time in his career, exerted his clout for personal reasons. Hence, no gossip to report. But Khushi had seen a gynaecologist. Babuji received her report, even before we could complete the fourth-day rituals for the dead."

Auntie Maya's unflinching eyes and the pragmatic way she narrated the events as if she had recounted the story hundreds of times, sent a shudder down Sami's spine.

A feeling of weariness, creeping slowly up her limbs, made Sami want to curl up on the living room carpet and slip away like one who loses consciousness, and upon waking, has no real memory of the past.

That Bali, the man whose ardent arms she had lain in, whose mouth she had kissed and whose face she had taken as a loving and lovable face, however briefly, could hurt someone so deeply that she was forced to end herself, was beyond her ken.

By the time Sami reached home, her mood shifted. She no longer wanted to sleep away her thoughts but to process, analyse and verbalize them with anyone who might listen. Of course, she instructed herself, she would not utter a word until either Amma or Babuji was ready.

To her surprise, it was Babuji who answered the door.

"Babuji!"

"Ah! Sami. Come in. Would you like a cup of coffee? Your Amma is resting."

247

"Can I just ask," said Sami, when she'd settled on the kitchen chair, "How is it you are getting the door and offering to make me coffee? Where are the servants?"

Babuji smiled and mussed her hair. "You haven't noticed? We have no maids anymore. Amma does not feel she can trust them after ... Khushi ... the lies and gossip they spread."

"But who does the cooking? And everything else?"

"Your mother cooks more often than not. We also use a food service. Good, home-cooked food delivered by some women's shelter. And a cleaning woman, who comes in twice a day."

Sami digested the information. So, there were new routines. How naïve of her to think that growth and change came only with leaving, and those left behind would remain as they were, strangled in habit.

It occurred to her, too, that like it or not, Khushi's passing had become the most significant event in their lives and time would forever be counted backwards Before Khushi or forwards After Khushi.

Her father was trying to draw her attention, waving a coffee mug in front of her face.

Sami smiled. "No, thank you. But I have one more question. If there are no maids, who is listening to that persistent, annoying music?"

Babuji sighed softly. "It's the silence. It gets to her. Your Amma has panic attacks sometimes. She says, the music helps her ... not think."

For a while, they sat quietly, lost in their own musings.

"I think, Babuji, I will have some coffee after all."

Her father rose from his chair. "Glad to have something to do. Glad to be of help."

She was in his room, waiting. Atal's face broke into a smile as wide as hope.

"Hello." He grinned, dropping his book bag with a thump.

"Wanna do something?"

He nodded. "Let me get changed, first."

They bounced a few ideas around. Movie? Ice-cream?

Scrabble? In the end, they simply stretched out, she on his bed, he on the carpet, exchanging endless reminiscences.

At last, after a brief pause, Sami asked, "Do you still miss her?"

He did not answer immediately. She loved that about her brother. How he paid attention, how he took his time before he responded to a question – with all the sincerity and kindness at his disposal.

"At first, a lot. Now, I miss the idea of her. Being around. Sitting at the family table. Growing older." He closed his eyes.

"Atal. I'm sorry."

"I missed you too, Sami." He said softly. "Sometimes I wasn't sure whether I was crying for her or you."

Night-time was reserved for herself. She missed Martin with an almost physical ache. And Patrick peeking from behind him. I will be back soon enough, my loves. Better. Stronger. You will see.

She turned the night light off. Sometimes it was nice to lie in absolute darkness. It made the sunrise so much more astonishing.

Summers in Mumbai were hot and humid. The ocean breeze did little to shake you out of your torpor. Sami, like the rest of the city, floated along in an aquamarine haze.

Then, one early morning, she awoke feeling different.

The feeling didn't go away when she located her bedroom

slippers, persisted when she went down for her first cup of tea and stayed with her when she trotted off to shower.

She slipped into a new skirt and in a girly moment decided to twirl. That is when she knew her limp was permanently gone!

She went down to join her parents for breakfast. How can I tell them of this little miracle without raking up the past? She was still revelling in this newfound freedom from pain, this sense of wellness when Amma took her hand in her own.

"Sami," she said, stroking the ring on her wedding finger. "Maya told us that you were married."

Sami swallowed.

"I was going to tell you ..."

"It is okay, Samar. You are a married woman now. Do ask him to come down." Babuji intervened.

"Babuji, are you sure?"

"Of course. Semper deinceps – ever forward. Besides, it is not right to stay away from your spouse for so many days." Babuji admonished.

"You are happy with him? He is a good man?" Amma asked, with a touch of nervousness.

"Yes, Amma. I am very happy. He is a good man. You will like him. Only ..."

"What, Sami?" There was panic in Amma's eyes. "Nothing! I mean... it's just ... he has a little boy too. Patrick. His son from a previous marriage." She held her breath.

Her parents nodded. Amma's nod went on a little longer.

"Is Patrick a good boy?"

Sami laughed. "Yes." She said, tenderly. "Yes, he's a good boy. He is like our Cheetah."

"Oyeeewah! Then, bring him home, Child! Bring him home, Little Amma!"

So, she did.

There is Help

You are not alone. Contact a suicide hotline if you need someone to talk to. If you have a friend in need of help, please encourage that person to contact a suicide hotline as well.

Acknowledgements

I believe this book would not have been written had these people not been in my life. Therefore:

I thank my parents – my beacons of light.

I thank you, my family, for your unconditional love. I got lucky.

Finally, I would be remiss if I did not thank the ghosts of countless writers who guide my hand and shape my inner world.